QUEEN MACBETH

Also by Val McDermid

A Place of Execution
Killing the Shadows
The Grave Tattoo
Trick of the Dark
The Vanishing Point

ALLIE BURNS NOVELS
1979
1989

LINDSAY GORDON NOVELS
Report for Murder
Common Murder
Final Edition
Union Jack
Booked for Murder
Hostage to Murder

KAREN PIRIE NOVELS
The Distant Echo
A Darker Domain
The Skeleton Road
Out of Bounds
Broken Ground
Still Life
Past Lying

TONY HILL/CAROL JORDAN NOVELS
The Mermaids Singing
The Wire in the Blood
The Last Temptation
The Torment of Others
Beneath the Bleeding
Fever of the Bone
The Retribution
Cross and Burn
Splinter the Silence
Insidious Intent
How the Dead Speak

KATE BRANNIGAN NOVELS
Dead Beat
Kick Back
Crack Down
Clean Break
Blue Genes
Star Struck

SHORT STORY COLLECTIONS
The Writing on the Wall
Stranded
Christmas is Murder
Gunpowder Plots (ebook only)

NON-FICTION
A Suitable Job for a Woman
Forensics
My Scotland

QUEEN MACBETH

A Novel

VAL McDERMID

Atlantic Monthly Press
New York

First published in Great Britain in 2024 by Polygon, an imprint of Birlinn Ltd.

Published simultaneously in Canada
Printed in the United States of America

First Grove Atlantic hardcover edition: September 2024

ISBN 978-0-8021-6429-2
eISBN 978-0-8021-6430-8

Typeset by 3btype, Edinburgh

Library of Congress Cataloging-in-Publication data is available for this title.

Atlantic Monthly Press
an imprint of Grove Atlantic
154 West 14th Street
New York, NY 10011

Distributed by Publishers Group West

groveatlantic.com

24 25 26 27 28 10 9 8 7 6 5 4 3 2 1

To my pal Linda Riley,
who knows all about being misrepresented!

Author's Note

There's a lot we don't know about the land north of Hadrian's Wall at the end of the tenth century. Partly that's because a vanishingly small number of people had access to ink and paper. And partly because those who did were more inclined towards copying religious texts than writing the medieval version of a blog.

But some things we do know. Macbeth and his lady were not the power-hungry bloody tyrants that Shakespeare wrote in his Scottish play. For a start, Macbeth wasn't even his name — it was Macbethad. His wife wasn't Lady Macbeth — she was Gruoch. If he couldn't get their names right, how can we trust anything else he tells us? I've left him as Macbeth, but I'm admitting up front that's for the sake of convenience.

We also know that when Macbeth killed Duncan — yes, he did kill Duncan, but it was on the field of battle, not in the dead of night when Duncan was a guest in his castle —

there was no such thing as Scotland. There was Moray and Alba and Dál Riata and Fife and a few other 'kingdoms'.

We also know, for example, there was no such thing as a direct line of succession. Your son would only succeed you as Thane, or Mormaer, or Earl if he had enough of an army to hold the throne. It helped if he'd had the good sense to marry a woman who would bring a solid alliance with her.

And so on. On the one hand, it's frustrating when there are so many more questions than answers. On the other hand, it leaves plenty of space for the imagination. And that's what I've enjoyed along the road to setting Shakespeare straight. I hope you enjoy discovering more about the incident-packed lives of Gruoch and Macbeth.

Any mistakes are uniquely mine.

QUEEN
MACBETH

Angus's feet always warn me of his coming. My women move with delicacy, steps barely whispering through the crushed oyster shells that line the path to our fastness. The monks always come in pairs, scuffing noisily to announce their arrival, as if to avoid any hint of impropriety towards us. I remain, in spite of everything, a queen.

But heavy-footed Angus pounds the shells to powder in his eagerness to be with us, to share whatever needs sharing. A successful hunting party on the shores of the loch, a new style of carving freshly arrived from a distant outpost of the Culdees, a far-off battle whose outcome will touch us not at all. It's all the same to Angus; it breaks the monotony of his days among the women.

He chaps at the door, mindful of his place. Ligach walks across, drop spindle in hand, twisting the fleece without pause. She spins her yarn with no apparent attention, her pattern of movement as regular as a tic, only with a more benevolent result. I have sometimes wondered whether she puts it to one side when she takes Angus to her bed. 'I think she must,' Aife says. 'Not even Ligach can spin on her back.' I am too fond of Aife to comment on her lack of imagination.

With an easy movement of her wrist, Ligach's thumb catches the latch and lets the door swing open. Angus's cheeks are pink above the thick russet of his beard, either from the cold March wind or from his haste to give us news. 'A boat,' he says. 'From the far shore.'

Not the short crossing, that narrow strait between us here on St Serf's Isle and the sheltered shore by the river mouth. No, Angus means the long way across Loch Leven. It's not as if nobody ever comes over to the monks from that direction, but it's not something that happens every day. Or even every week.

'And yesterday was St Patrick's Day,' he says quickly, eager to make his point. It's a point that eludes us at first. We exchange looks, faces blank.

'Remember?' He's got the wind behind him now, sure that for once he has the higher ground. He moves further into the room, his heavy tread filling the air with puffs of the incense smell of the holy grass, freshly spread only yesterday. 'Eithne said a holy day would bring danger for the king.'

Eithne's face clears. 'Malcolm,' she says. 'Remember? His men passed on the far side of the loch on their way north. I told you, he was making for Scone to prevent your son being anointed king.'

Angus nods eagerly.

'And I told *you* he was far too late. By more than half a year.' I generally speak softly to Eithne but there are times when even the generosity of long friendship slips.

'She did say he wouldn't succeed,' Aife reminds me.

'Not then, not the coronation,' Eithne continues, serene as she always is when she's convinced she knows a truth none of the rest of us has access to. 'But it's not too late for Malcolm to end your son's rule. I said Lulach would lose his throne on a holy day.' *Like St Patrick's Day*, the unspoken words hanging heavy between us.

I turn from her and wrap my zybeline stole more closely around me. I step past Angus and through the door. Tears spring from my eye, forced by the bitter wind. It blows from the land where I grew up, where I sat on the throne alongside Macbeth for seventeen years. I have not been back since the day of the battle that robbed me of the love of my life; this is the place where I have spent my sorrow. Today, I expect nothing but more grief from that quarter.

I stare out past the slender pines and the sharp marram grass to the choppy water of the loch. My eyes are not as sharp as they were, but the boat is drawing nearer against the wind and I think I can make out two passengers huddled on the thwart, hunched shoulder to shoulder.

I return to our haven and settle on the tall carved chair the monks made for my husband when he became king, in honour of the support and succour he had always given them. No matter that they had heard the reports that his path to the throne was dappled with blood; they judged him by the actions they saw for themselves. They were as much Macbeth's men as they were God's. And still they honour his memory.

Aife crosses to the rear of the room and moves the curtain of beaten deerskin aside. She beckons Eithne to the window. 'Come here. Tell me what you see.'

When she's wholly present, Eithne uses her eyes in the
same way the rest of us do. It's likely what saved her from
being drowned a witch, that gift of being able to move
between vision and reality. She leans into Aife. 'Aye. A
coble with two men not at the oars. Soldiers, I'd say. Heads
bowed.' She swivels round to face me. 'Gruoch, this will be
a sad day.'

I've already made that reckoning. 'Not Malcolm's men,
then.'

'He's still ignorant of your whereabouts.' Never one to
hold back, Angus says what we'd all like to believe.
'Otherwise he'd have stopped on his way north.' Unspoken,
something like, *to deal with you.* I may only be queen in
name, but memories are long in these lands. Mine is still a
name men would rally behind; Malcolm is shrewd enough
to realise that, and to fear it.

'Our king knows we're biding here,' Aife says, defiant.
'He would not betray his mother.'

I shake my head. 'My son is a man like any other.
If Lulach thought it was the way to an easier
outcome, I would not think less of him if he gave us up.
But I think he will not.'

'He has never been a bonnie fechter.' Ligach's tone is
tart.

Ever loyal, Angus scoffs. 'Lulach is a true king.'

'And I am still a true queen of the royal line, not just
the mother of the king,' I remind him. 'That is my value to

Lulach and to Malcolm. Macbeth taught me a game when he first came from Mull. He called it *fidchell*. It was a game of capture and conquest. The most powerful piece on the board was the queen. My son learned the game at Macbeth's knee, its tactics and its ploys. Lulach would never give up his queen.'

The first time I set eyes on Macbeth, I knew he was the very pattern of manhood. Not simply that he was well-set and even-featured, though that was no mark against him. But although he was a little lower in rank than the man I was wedded to, he seemed more like a lord than Gille Coemgáin. My husband was Mormaer of Moray, king of the north in all but name, Macbeth merely his cousin, bound to his side by blood and honour. All I knew of him before we came face to face was that his name meant son of life and that his men called him Deircc, the Red One. I assumed it was because his blade was drenched with blood.

I had not considered that it might refer to his fox-red hair. He looked like a man on fire, his eyes blazing blue as the heart of a lump of ice on a high moor. When his eyes settled on me, I knew he saw beyond Gille Coemgáin's wife to the woman I was meant to be. But when my father had made a trade of me to Gille Coemgáin, I had no choice. They allowed me to keep my three women with me, but only because they believed them to be powerless. That's a mistake men have made too often around women.

The night Macbeth came among us, Eithne lit the candles in our quarters, then burned sage and bog myrtle and another sweet herb whose name none of us knew. We lay dreamy and drowsing on the furs Gille Coemgáin allowed us as a mark of his power and status, waiting for Eithne to reach the place she speaks from. 'He will be the one. He will surely plant a king.'

Her words sent a chill through me. It had been seventeen moons since the wedding and still there was no sign of an heir for Gille Coemgáin. Not for want of trying on his part. Aife, always sharp-witted, said my womb likely refused his seed because I had no love for him, and she may have been right. I was not so foolish as to resist his attempts to get a son on me, but it was only ever my body that was present; my mind was elsewhere, in the woods and the shorelines of our land. Never in the bed with him.

And it's true there was not much to love about Gille. He lived to eat and drink well, and that had coarsened the good looks he'd been blessed with. There was no tenderness in him; he was uncaring and rough, always putting his own needs and desires first. He had a high opinion of his qualities and his standing; he saw in me only a reflection of his own status. He trusted advice from no one, regardless of their experience or proven good sense. Gille always knew best.

And it appeared to have worked to his benefit. After the savage murder of Macbeth's father, his kingdom had been divided between Malcolm in Alba and Gille Coemgáin in Moray.

Macbeth might have hoped to become Mormaer of Moray, but sons don't always succeed their fathers if they don't have an army at their back. Lacking land, lacking support, lacking a wife of the royal blood trumped his place in the line of inheritance.

After the murder of Findlaich, Macbeth's father, there ran a fleet-footed rumour that Gille and Malcolm were responsible. It was hard not to suspect them of a conspiracy when both benefited so. But my husband had always denied it, and it seemed Macbeth accepted that. Now he had come to pay due respect. To put his small army at our disposal, were the English or the Vikings to visit. So, of course, there was a celebration. Gille had to lay on a feast that Macbeth could never hope to equal if we took it on ourselves to venture across the sea to his hall in Mull.

There was roast lamb, wild boar and venison. Sides of salmon and sea trout, smoked fish and mussels. Porridge sweetened with apples baked in honey and sweet cicely. Bannocks and bread made from the flour of oats and beans. Roasted turnips and onions, tiny sharp radishes and sauces from mustard balls. Stewed plums with crushed roasted *hazelnuts. Cheese and curds. Me at his side in my finest robes.*

And, of course, strong ale and barley bree to set heads bleezing.

No expense had been spared, no stores left unplundered. Bellies would be grumbling with hunger to pay for this display of wealth. Not my belly, of course, nor my three women. Not Gille's either. But the others who depended on what came from our kitchen – they'd be going to bed with their stomachs empty for a couple of weeks till the larder was replenished.

Then the filidh took the floor with his usual bardic fervour. A tale of battle, told to the hypnotic rhythm of a tattoo on the bodhran. As the story reached its climax, Macbeth leapt on the table and laid a pair of crossed swords at his feet. 'Give me music,' he shouted, and the piper answered with a reel that made my head swirl.

Not Macbeth. He raised his hands above his head, fingers imitating a stag's antlers, and began to dance. His feet moved among the four quarters made by the blades so nimbly it became impossible to keep track of how he got there and where he would go next. His lèine was dyed madder red and it danced with him, rising above his knees, giving us flashes of his woad-blue braies. And his hair like a flame. I'd never seen a display of colour like it. He danced like a man possessed. Even Aife, who has no interest in men, flushed pink at the excitement of it.

He reached the end with a flourish and made a deep bow to Gille, then to me. He jumped down from the table; his men surrounded him and shouted his name. I saw a brief flash of resentment cross my husband's face. Clearly Macbeth had not heard how Gille liked to be the name given most praise, especially after a display of luxury such as we'd laid on that night.

Before my husband could glimpse the thoughts Macbeth's display had set running, I excused myself and slipped out of the hall, Aife and Eithne at my heels. 'You had better return,' I said. 'Don't give Gille occasion to make you the butt of his anger.'

They understood my reasoning. No matter what I felt towards Gille, I was bound by my father's insistence. He himself was the son of a king, which made me part of that same royal line. So he could countenance nothing less than the highest rank for me. Mormaer of Moray, king in all but name of the Highland fiefdom, was the perfect match. A marriage with Gille Coemgáin would make stronger my father's position and do him honour. Never mind that Gille had a bloodstained history and a jealous temper. I was traded for status. Not the first nor the last woman to be treated like a gaming piece

I placed but one condition on the deal. I insisted that my three women should remain at my side. Eithne, for her understanding of the world we cannot see; Aife, for the support and sustenance she gives Eithne's gift, and thus to *all four of us; and Ligach, ever practical, who never sees a problem, only a challenge. They have been my companions since childhood, and I knew I would struggle at Gille's court without my three allies at my back.*

Of course, Gille distrusted them and missed no opportunity to treat them harshly. He could not attack me directly, for my father's name still carried weight even in Gille's territories. So he made them surrogates. If he had noticed me leaving the feast accompanied by Aife and Eithne, he would take out his wounded pride on them.

I watched them return to the hall, arm in arm in the pearly moonlight, then made my way to the physic garden Eithne and Aife had created. It was fragrant and soothing, the night scents different from the day. I breathed deeply and felt my turbulent heart return to its regular beat.

But the turmoil followed me.

Eithne keeps watch as the boat draws nearer to the shore, pitching and tossing against the hilly horizon. I don't envy them the journey. 'I don't recognise them,' she says. If anyone else spoke with such certainty, we'd scoff, for who among us can be sure of recognition from the back of men's heads? But Eithne sees differently.

'Away up to the monastery, Angus,' I say. 'Tell the abbot

to fetch them up to the refectory and feed them. Stick by his side. Your very presence will keep him honest.'

'What about the others?' Aife demands, anxious.

'The monks will follow his lead. They have obedience bred into them.'

'Even Brother Brendan?' Eithne says.

We exchange looks. From anyone else, it would be a casual enough comment. From Eithne, it's a warning. A reminder that Brother Brendan is a thorn in the side of the abbot, a law unto himself who questions every instruction and holy precept in his thick Irish brogue. He has no malice in him, but he has never approved of our presence here. 'Women are a temptation to our chastity,' he once said to me. 'Even crones like you.' Scornful, I laughed, and he laughed with me. But I could hear the unease that lay beneath.

Angus already has his hand on the latch. His face is a question, directed at me.

Ligach speaks. 'Send Brother Brendan here, Angus. Tell him I need help with the hives. He loves the bees.'

'He loves the honey more,' Aife points out.

'We'll stop his mouth with honey. Eithne, you have what you need to hand?'

She's already on her way across to the carved oak chest my brother made for her before he was murdered. It's two trays deep. The top level contains the everyday herbs, the ointments and tinctures she uses to treat common ailments such as coughs and afflictions of the skin. The lower level is not for the eyes or hands of anyone less skilled than Eithne. That means almost anyone in the whole country.

'White poppy and henbane,' she says, lifting out the top tray and removing two lambskin pouches from beneath. Eithne passes through the deerskin curtain to the cubbyhole where she prepares her concoctions. We are so still now I can hear the grinding of mortar and pestle.

She emerges and takes down a new flask of mead. 'I was keeping this for a celebration,' she says, sadness in her voice.

'If we survive tonight, that will be worth celebrating,' Ligach says, her voice sharp.

'The boat's at the shore,' Aife reports.

We fall silent again, watching Eithne pouring a beaker of mead, adding more honey, then tipping in what looks like a very small amount of powder. I can't believe it will suffice, but I'm not about to start doubting her capabilities.

I move across to the window and stand behind Aife's shoulder. Should anyone look, I'd be no more than an outline. Beyond the window are the carefully tended clusters of plants that Eithne has been cultivating since we fled here after that last battle sent us into exile. Her skills in diagnosis and treatment have paid our way, more even than the endowment of the monastery land Macbeth and I made years ago.

The two passengers gather their cloaks, tucking them into the rope belts at their waists. I see the glint of steel.

And a long streak of red brown from shoulder to waist on one of them.

Soldiers, then. Not simply messengers. They clamber over the side of the boat and splash through thigh-deep cold loch water. Neither of their faces is familiar to me, but Aife says, 'The tall one? He's the youngest Seaton boy. His father waited on your husband, Gruoch. Surely he'll not be one of Malcolm's men.'

I wish I had her certainty. After Lumphanen, after the battle when my heart broke, I doubt everything and everyone.

Then the abbot appears, habit hitched to his knees, almost running across the machair to the sandy beach, the sharp sea grasses whipping his bare calves. I've never seen him move so fast. The cantor is at his heels, Angus bringing up the rear. They stop short of embracing the strangers, but it's clear the encounter is a welcome. A wary welcome, but a welcome nonetheless.

And then a mighty battering at the door startles us. My heart almost stops, but Eithne remains self-possessed. 'Brendan,' she says calmly. 'Aife, let him in.'

I moved between the clusters of plants, running my fingers along stems of rosemary and lavender that lined the path.

Their familiar fragrance calmed me; Eithne said it allayed the superstitions of those who think she's a witch. I wasn't so sure about that; I thought what stilled the tongues of those who would denounce her was the protection our royal throne granted her. Everyone knew it would be an act of folly to accuse the handmaiden of the Mormaer's wife of witchery. It grieved me to owe anything to Gille, but I had him to thank for that. I suspect he did it out of fear rather than love; Eithne unsettles even the most battle-hardened men with those eyes that seem to see straight through them to the far shore of their nightmares.

And she had unsettled me that night, with her impossible implication that Macbeth would be the one to give me a son. Even to think that was dangerous beyond comprehension. If she'd made such a prophecy in the hearing of Gille Coemgáin, the Mormaer of Moray, the husband of Gruoch, nothing would have saved her. Or the rest of us, in all likelihood. Me, Aife, Ligach – we'd all have gone down together with Eithne.

Deep in thought, I walked on, trying to make sense of my reaction to Macbeth. I'd seen handsome men before, though not many so easy on the eye. I'd heard fluent-tongued men before, though not many with his quickness of wit. I'd even seen dancers with such abandon and flair before, though few with such finely turned legs. But there was something that marked him out and I seemed unable to put a name to it.

'Unable or unwilling?' I suspected Aife would have asked, a tease in her voice to temper the temerity of her response.

Before I could find the answer, I heard quick footsteps at my back. Cursing my recklessness, I swivelled round, reaching for the brooch at my shoulder. Its pin was long and sharp; I learned from my mother the importance of always having some defence to hand.

I turned and faced the very danger that was troubling my thoughts. Macbeth slowed to a halt a few feet away from me. He spread his hands to show he was unarmed, though I was not convinced. He was too careful, too clever to enter another man's hall without something to protect against the fickleness of alliances. At the very least, there must have been a dagger concealed somewhere about his person.

He smiled, dipping his head in acknowledgement of my status. 'My lady Gruoch. I hope I didn't startle you. I came outside for air and I saw you among these plants here.' Not quite apologetic, not quite flirtatious. But somewhere in the middle.

I scolded myself for the blush I felt rising from my neck. Then I told myself it didn't matter, that the moonlight would obscure a response I couldn't afford. 'One of my women grows them for the pot. And for their healing qualities.' I sounded stiff and formal to my own ears, which was definitely the safest path for me.

His smile quirked into something more mischievous.
'Is she the one they say is a witch?'

I frowned. 'They would not utter such lies in my
hearing. Eithne is a wise woman with rare gifts in tending
the sick. There is no magic in that, just an understanding
of how plants work hand in hand with our bodies.'

He nodded. 'For we are all one with nature, if we can
only decipher the complicated bonds. I have such a
herbalist back on Mull. Your Eithne is one to keep close
and keep safe.'

'She is. As you have a gift for the dance, so has she for
the plants.' The words were out before I knew it. The
man brought a dose of cac-shiubhal from my lips.

'You enjoyed my dance?' He performed a quick set
of steps.

'Perhaps not as much as you did.'

He was not at all put out of countenance. A wry
expression flitted across his features, and he gestured to
the fallen beech trunk that Aife had persuaded two of
Gille's wood carvers to turn into a crude bench. 'I love
the dance, I can't deny that. That yoking together of
precision and euphoria. But my legs are tired now. Shall
we sit a while?'

'I do not make a habit of sitting with strange men in
dark gardens,' I said, stiff as I could manage.

'But I am not strange, I am a kinsman. I think we
share . . . what is it? A grandfather? A great-grandfather?'

He settled on the bench as if it were shaped to his body.

'We share a darker blood.' I sat at the other end of the bench, studying his face in the moonlight. It threw a dramatic cast on his features, silvering the vivid red of his hair. I rebuked myself for the thought, but I couldn't help wondering what it would be like to run my hands through its thick waves.

'Findlaich.' His merriment had disappeared, his mouth a thin slash across his beard. 'Is it true, then, what they say? That your husband's hands are red with the blood of my father?'

I looked away. I did not want to meet that blue stare without the warmth I'd seen in it a few moments ago. 'Is that what you believe? Did you come here to test your conviction?'

'I did not grow up alongside Gille. I don't know him like a cousin or a brother. So I can't be sure when he is lying to me. Coming here at the head of an armed band, taking an eye for an eye – that would have been the choice of some of those closest to me. But that way, I could never be certain I was killing the right man. So I chose to come as a friend so I could learn to judge for myself.'

I turned to face him again. His face was sombre, the animation put away for future use. 'I can be of no help to you in that quest. My husband does not confide in me about matters of strategy.'

He gave an impatient shake of the head. 'No, no. You

misjudge me. I was not trying to provoke a betrayal from you.' He looked away. 'I apologise, I should not have spoken so freely.' A frown. 'I don't know why I . . .'

'I'm the one who raised the matter. I appreciate your frankness. In our hall, my women and I have to assume the role of spies to find out what is happening.'

His eyes returned to my face. 'That must feel . . . strange?'

'It feels necessary. Choices are made that affect our lives. Sometimes a matter of life and death. Even if we have no right to be part of the decisions, I think we have a right to know the outcomes. My father was the most traditional of men, yet he was willing to explain himself to me.' I shrugged. 'It seldom changed anything if I disagreed. But at least I knew what was coming for me.'

'When I marry, I like to think I would be more like your father than your husband.' He shook his head, an expression of disgust on his face. 'Listen to me. "When I marry." I have little enough to offer a woman. The disregarded son of a murdered father who has not even managed to revenge his death.'

'Better to be slow than to shed innocent blood, surely?'

'Not all of my kinsmen see things that way. I have to tread a careful path.'

I couldn't help smiling. 'Judging by your footwork between the swords, that should come naturally.'

He smiled too, and I noticed his shoulders relax.
'I plan to survive, my lady.'

I dared. 'I hope you do.' And the small voice in the
back of my head wondered whether talking thus to me
was part of that survival strategy.

He rose, wincing a little as his back straightened.
'I must go back. Gille will mistrust my absence.'

'Mine also. The advantage I have is that we women
can always fall back on the ailments of our sex.'

He chuckled. 'I have enjoyed our conversation.
Perhaps we can talk again?'

'How long do you plan to stay?'

He was on his feet, looking around, checking for
watchful eyes. We had been partially sheltered by the
surrounding plants, but a warrior takes nothing for
granted. 'We will be here for two or three weeks
perhaps,' he said. 'Cousin Gille has some days' hunting
planned. He wants to show off how plentiful the game
larder of these hills is. To remind me that I am the poor
relation.' That wry glance again.

'There's more than one kind of richness.' I had no
idea where this boldness came from; I had seen too many
bad outcomes for women who were careless. I was
generally the most careful of women.

His eyes met mine in a level stare. 'I hope to find that
out for myself.' Then, in a swift movement, he reached
for my hand and brought it to his lips. They were cool

and dry against my fingers, but when he withdrew, I felt as if I'd been branded. 'Till the next time,' he said and disappeared into the shadows like a ghost.

He'd barely gone when Ligach slipped out from a cluster of fennel as tall as she. 'Well played, Gruoch,' she said, head to one side, considering.

'I had no game in mind,' I protested. 'I was simply conversing with our guest.'

She raised her eyebrows, amusement lifting the corners of her generous mouth. 'If Eithne is right, then there is a game to be played.'

I stood up and faced her. 'Eithne is not always clear – and not always right.'

Ligach linked her arm in mine, and we moved back through the garden towards the hall. 'But if she is right . . . this is a game you might enjoy?'

Any reply would have held me hostage, so I said nothing.

Not that night.

Aife lifts the latch and Brother Brendan lurches in. His tonsure still reveals stubble black as sea coal from Fife, and his dark eyes conceal more than they reveal. He's a big man, and clumsy with it, except when he's helping Eithne with the bees. Then, he becomes a delicate creature, his fat fingers handling the honeycombs with an unexpected tenderness that protects the honey and the wax walls of the cells. It's true that he loves the honey, but he also seems to love the bees. It goes both ways – Eithne says he has never been stung, that the bees crawl on his arms but don't sting him. Aife says he's so thick-skinned he doesn't notice, but none of us takes her literally.

He stops a couple of steps into the barn. He always makes sure to keep his distance from us, as if being closer than a spear's length will drive him wild with untameable lust. 'Angus says you need help with the hives?' he says, his voice a deep rumble in his chest.

'I want to move the one by the wall back alongside the one nearest the barn,' Eithne says. Then she points to the beaker on the table near him, meanwhile pouring another four beakers from the special bottle. 'But first we should celebrate the arrival of visitors. We don't often see strangers, and I've been saving this bottle for a special occasion.' She lifts one of the beakers and raises it in a toast. The rest of us follow her lead and call out the ancient Gaelic toast, 'Slàinte mhath!'

Brendan wastes no time in yielding to temptation. He lifts his brimming beaker and takes off half of it in a single draught. He wipes his mouth on the sleeve of his cassock and smacks his lips. 'Praise be to God,' he exclaims. 'Eithne, you have excelled yourself! You'd make the Blessed

Virgin herself turn to drink.' He takes another slurp. 'Magnificent,' he says.

We all murmur agreement and it's no lie. The mead is sweet and rich, but with a fragrant and elusive quality that sets it apart from Eithne's usual offerings. She pushes the bottle towards Brendan. It's untainted by her concoction, but it's still a strong brew. Brendan tops up his beaker and swallows another gargantuan swig while we merely sip at the small ration Eithne has allowed us.

'Tha's . . . tha's ambro . . . ambaro . . . amborsio . . .' he slurs, burping. Then giggles. Then another gulp. 'Witchcroft . . . I mean, wishcraft . . . not that, youse arenae . . .' Then a crash as he goes over like a felled tree, taking two stools with him.

'He'll be out for hours now,' Eithne says, clearly pleased with herself.

'Are you sure?' I ask.

Eithne scoffs. 'The apothecaries in Rome told me they use it to render patients insensible so they can perform all kinds of surgeries. From what I heard, we could cut his leg off and he wouldn't notice.'

'All the same, should we tie him up?' Ligach asks, studying him from various angles.

'Roll him into the corner,' I suggest. 'When he wakes up, he'll believe he's just having the world's worst hangover.'

So, heaving and grunting, and cursing too, we manage to manoeuvre big Brother Brendan into the far corner of the room, among the pile of fleeces Ligach hasn't got round to spinning yet. By now, he's snoring. Thankfully, the pigs are penned between the barn and the abbey; they'll get the blame if the snores make it as far as the monks' cells.

'Now what do we do?' Aife asks.

'We wait,' I tell them.

'For what?' Ligach next. I hear a nervousness in her voice that's not like her.

'For as long as it takes for Angus to come back with news. And in the meantime, Eithne can burn some herbs and see what answers she can give us before we decide what questions to ask.'

The morning after Macbeth's dance found Gille in a dark mood. He sent for me while most of his men were sleeping off the effects of the barley bree and the women were still working around the snoring sprawl of Macbeth's men to clear the worst of the mess from the hall.

I found him in his chamber, still in his nightshirt. My heart sank; a summons like this usually meant he was set on another attempt to get a son on me. But that morning he wanted something different.

He gestured to a settle, half-occupied by his discarded

banqueting robes. They stank of smoke and sweat and cooked meat. 'What do you make of our cousin, wife?'

I sat down, arranging myself to best advantage. I had to tread carefully. I knew I must not appear to have taken the wrong kind of interest in Macbeth. 'He seems amiable,' I said. 'Better to dance than be quarrelsome, as some of our cousins can be.'

Gille ruminated, chewing the ends of his moustache. 'You know some men say I was behind the death of Findlaich?'

Time to flatter. 'If you had wanted to murder Findlaich, you would not have hidden behind the hands of other men. You would have faced him directly and the world would know it.'

He smiled. 'You know me well. But Macbeth does not. Do you think he believes the rumour?'

'There is no sign of hostility from him or his men. They are not heavily armed. They didn't pick fights when they were drunk. They just got more drunk and more cheerful. They seem to be without guile.'

'Aye, but they could have stashed their weapons nearby before they arrived. They could be lulling us to sleep, persuading us to drop our guard. Then falling on us in our beds and gutting us. Taking their revenge for the hurt they think we caused them.'

I allowed myself a low chuckle. 'They're not that subtle, Gille. Macbeth has few fully-fledged warriors at his back. *These lads are barely one step up from peasants. If that had been their plan, they could have moved on us last night. Half our men are still insensible after their excesses. You were generous to allow them to indulge themselves so much.'*

'Not all of them,' he smirked. 'I picked ten of my best fighters, men I can trust. I ordered them to act like drunken ruffians, but to remain sober. To watch Macbeth and his men, to discover whether they were also pretending. When the carousing was over, they reported that the visitors were sincerely and thoroughly pished.'

'There you go. They're only here to pay tribute and have a good time at someone else's expense.'

He shook his head. 'I wish I could believe that.' He pushed himself upright, dragging a wolfskin across his shoulders. 'What does your woman say?' He looked away, not meeting my eyes. He hated to admit there might be some substance to Eithne's utterances. It was an insult to his manhood, to need that reassurance.

If I'd been foolish enough to answer him honestly, Gille would have made sure not one of Macbeth's company was left standing. It would have become a tale of hospitality betrayed that reverberated throughout Moray and Alba; it would have given Malcolm the perfect excuse to march on us. But since my marriage I'd grown proficient at lying; I'd had plenty of practice. 'Eithne says Macbeth comes in a spirit of goodwill towards Moray.'

'To Moray? Not to me?' He snapped back to stare at
my face.

'Moray is you, my lord. And you stand for your entire
kingdom. Any man who hurts Moray hurts you, you
know that.' A wary nod from Gille. 'And so it follows
that goodwill towards Moray is goodwill towards you.
If I thought Eithne's words meant anything different,
I would have come direct to you. I wouldn't have waited
till you asked me.' I got up from the settle and joined
him on the bed.

Time to be the devoted wife.

Brendan's snoring is more subdued, thankfully. Against the
background rumble, Aife prepares dinner. We dare not
light the cooking fire; this barn is supposed not to be
occupied, and we will take no chances of telltale smoke
while there are strangers on the isle. But there are the
remains of a ham and some lentil pottage which is as tasty
cold. We have vegetables pickled by Aife last summer, and
oatcakes. We will not go hungry.

Whether we will feel like eating is another matter. We
are all taut as bowstrings primed to loose our arrows into
the hearts of our enemies. Ligach paces the floor, tablet-
weaving a belt, its pattern a sequence of perfect chevrons

in shades of cream and brown. When the world ends and we are all made perfect, Ligach will still be weaving, only with gold and silver threads.

Eithne sits cross-legged, obsessively shuffling and rolling her runes. What she sees there she does not share. I'm glad she's keeping her own counsel, though I fear it's because all she can see is bad news. At last, she sits back on her heels and replaces her runes in their soft calfskin pouch. Her face gives nothing away.

We pick at our food, ears alert for any sound. Brendan drones on, now muttering softly every few minutes.

'Is he waking?' I ask.

Eithne shakes her head. 'Dreaming. He's lost in his past, dredging up old loves and losses. The poppy works on us like that – it takes us to a healing place where we can mend the old wounds that still trouble us. That's why it's so seductive, so addictive. Why I am careful not to give too much too often.'

There have been times when I would have loved that sweet release from pain, but I'm grateful she never led me down that path. In the torture grip of childbirth, I screamed for its release, and she refused, though I could see even at the time it was a hard choice for her. But her refusal also scares me – it means she believes there are worse pains that may yet come to afflict me. I did not think there could be worse griefs to bear than losing Macbeth.

After Aife decides that we've all given up on eating, she

clears the food away and we retreat to the main bedchamber. It has no windows, so we can have some light without betraying our presence. Together, we snuggle like puppies, a bumpy tumulus of furs that always brings us comfort when we need it. We're all tired after the heart-stopping moments of the day, but none of us is ready for sleep. The presentiment of worse to come keeps us all sharply awake.

'I feel a tingling in my thumbs,' Eithne says. 'Like when you touch the hairs on a nettle leaf. It's a warning that something bad is on its way.'

Ligach gives an exasperated sigh. 'That's not helpful, Eithne. We all know the men in the boat are not messengers of joy. A small child could tell that from the slump of their shoulders and the heaviness of their steps. Vague hints about wickedness only make me more anxious.'

'Don't.' Aife leaps to the defence of her love, ever loyal. 'She tells us what she senses, she doesn't choose it. You welcome it when it's news that suits you, but we don't get to pick and choose. We want the good, we have to live with the bad.'

Ligach harrumphs and shifts away from Aife and towards me.

'This isn't the time for squabbling like chickens in the yard,' I tell them. 'Whatever is coming for us, we need to face it with a solid front. I am your queen, and you are my shield in battle. We may not always agree, but we are as one. We stand together, rise or fall.'

Grunts of agreement from all three. We can't help feeling fear, but we can take strength from each other. After the battle at Lumphanen, when I lost Macbeth and we all lost so much of our lives, it was my women who stood at my side and my back, not armed warriors. When my beloved's regent arrived hotfoot from the battle with the news and the instruction that I must escape into exile, I wanted instead to rage at the heavens and run to kill Malcolm with my own hands. But my faithful trio wrapped me in their stalwart courage and bore me away here, where they knew I would find protection.

I remember that now, and know that however tightly wound fear has made us, we can still survive. We are like the screw on the arbalest, our courage wound to the sticking place, refusing to bend or break.

The sound of the latch is barely loud enough to be heard above Brendan's noises and through the wooden walls of our chamber, but we are all so familiar with it that we identify it at once. I scramble to my feet, Aife to my left, Eithne to my right, as Ligach strides for the inner door.

If this is the end, we will face it together.

I'm told some men are so drained by the act of houghmagandie that they fall fast asleep as soon as they've

spilled their seed, sometimes while their exhausted pintle is still inside their woman. Not so Gille Coemgáin. For him, a fuck always acted as an alarum. No sooner had he grunted his way to the end of his efforts than he'd leap to his feet as sudden as if he'd been stabbed in the buttocks by a ram's horn. Maybe that's why he never managed to plant a bairn in my womb – men are supposed to be emptied out by a fuck, but Gille reacted like a man whose energy had been filled to the brim.

There were never words of tenderness or even thanks for me. I might as well have been a whore for all the closeness we shared in the bedroom. He'd spread my legs and plunge in like a beast. I learned to use my own fingers to ease his passage after the first few times when he left me sore and bruised. A welcome lesson from Aife, who knows better than most what spares a woman from the worst.

At least our morning-after fuck took his mind off whatever Eithne might have seen in the runes. He pulled off his nightshirt without a word, wiped himself on its tail, and dressed for the hunt in his finest leather jerkin and breeches of warm woollen cloth Ligach had woven.

'Where will you take Macbeth today?' I asked.

'Braga tells me there are deer to be had in the river wood. Better on the north bank than on this side, but I'm not going to let him at the best of our hunting on the first day.' He gave a cunning smile. 'Let him work for it.'

'Work for it how?'

He cinched his belt over his generous belly. 'He needs
to show me he's worthy of the best chase. I want to see
whether he's got fire in his belly or just in his legs.
Otherwise he can fuck off back to Mull with his troop of
jessies.' He paused on his way out, eyeing me from head
to foot. 'Still a fine pair of dugs on you, Gruoch. About
time they were put in the service of my bairn.'

He'd started making comments like this more often.
It was unsettling. I know too many stories of infertile
wives cast aside – or worse. And there were no secrets in
our hall. Men had begun to snigger behind his back,
women to raise their eyebrows at my monthly courses.
Sooner or later some child would repeat a bawdy couplet
without understanding its meaning and his humiliation
would put a number on my days.

I watched from his window as they rode out to the
hunt, Macbeth and Gille at the head. The blaze of red a
contrast to the midnight black. Slowly, I dressed and
walked back across the yard to my room, head held high.
Aife looked up from kneading bread as I entered. It's not
really something she should have been undertaking; we
had cooks and bakers for such mundane tasks. But there
was no denying her bread tasted lighter and fresher than
anybody else's. So she supplied our top table in spite of
the master baker's muttering that there must be
witchcraft involved. Thankfully, he was known as a girnie
auld fool, so nobody paid attention.

But if I were to lose my place . . . Eithne would be open to allegations of dealing with dark forces. She and Aife would be accused of unnatural practices. And Ligach? She has a way with animals. The hounds love her; when the ewes are screaming with a difficult delivery, she calms them and births the lambs. Neither the huntsman nor the shepherds appreciated her skills. They'd happily have taken the losses of a few extra lambs to avoid being shown up.

Living with such anxiety was draining us. Something had to change.

The next thing we hear is the unmistakable call of a tawny owl – or rather Angus's version of it. He uses it to identify himself or to warn us of danger. We exchange looks of uncertainty. Which is it?

Ligach inches the door open just as Angus reaches it, almost knocking her off her feet as he breenges in. She gives him a light punch on the shoulder. 'Fool, you nearly stopped my heart.'

He raises his hands, pretending to stave off an attack. 'How else was I to warn you it was me and not somebody you'd be a lot less pleased to see?'

'What have you learned?' I demand. 'Come, sit with us

and tell everything.'

He does as he is told, settling cross-legged and solemn-faced at the end of the bed. Ligach leans into him, head against his arm. 'My lady, my queen. The news . . . the news is as bad as it could be. Malcolm marched his army north and met with King Lulach and his men at Strathbogie.'

'That's a long march,' Aife mutters. 'Malcolm wasn't giving up.'

Angus takes a deep breath. 'Lulach fought hard but the numbers were against him. My queen, his men were routed and the king . . . the king is dead.'

His words strike like an arrow of ice in my chest. I thought I had prepared myself for this. But nothing prepares a mother for the death of her child. It runs counter to the natural order; why should I be alive when my son is food for the crows on some distant battlefield? I was already mourning one king; now I must shed tears over a second. Was it not enough that Lulach's father had died defending our land? How much of our blood did Malcolm crave? It stabbed me to the very heart.

When Eithne had warned me that Malcolm intended to prevent my son's coronation, I understood her to mean the wider sense of his kingship. I refused to believe it although a deeper part of me understood he might yet lose his throne and his life. Now that I must face it, I feel a strange calm. The worst has happened. Nothing can hurt me more than this, and yet I am still alive, still breathing.

Still able to speak. 'So these men – they're not from Lulach's army? They're from Malcolm?'

Angus swallows hard and nods. 'Aye, my lady.'

'Are they searching for me?'

He looks ready to burst into tears. 'Malcolm knows Moray would rally behind you if you sent out the call—'

'There's damn all left to rally now.' Aife utters the bitter truth we all know.

Angus glowers at her but continues. 'He's sent out scouts across Moray and into Alba and Dál Riata with a price on your head. The two who arrived here today – they're one of those search parties.'

'Are they here out of obligation or do they really think we might be here?'

Angus shrugs. 'They know of the long-standing connection between you and Macbeth and the abbey here. The granting of the land. That's why they were sent here first. But they're not acting as if they expect to find you here. More that they're doing what they've been ordered. They told the abbot they will continue to Abernethy tomorrow if he can give them horses.'

I sense a collective breathing out. All we have to do now is be still and wait till morning. Aife and Eithne embrace, Angus puts an arm round Ligach, and I am the only one with both hands free when the door swings open.

The hunting party were gone for most of the day. It was impossible to tell from that alone whether it had been a good day or a bad; we were all four of us on edge, bad-tempered with each other, glum and restless. Dusk had almost faded into darkness when we heard the soft thud of hooves on the hard-packed earth inside the palisade. I left my quarters to greet them, my women at my back.

As soon as they reached the glow of the courtyard, we saw we could all relax. They were obviously in high spirits, Macbeth and Gille at the head of the unruly troop, all grinning satisfaction and comradeship. Behind them, bumping along in the wake of their dray horses, came the slipes carrying their spoils. As they drew level with us, we could see a pile of stags and hinds. Nothing unusual there. But pride of place went to a pair of wild boars, one massive and bloodied from the hunt, the other trimmer and likely younger. Its meat would be tender enough to roast directly on the fire; the other would require Eithne's skill with her herbs and the brewer's finest cider to bring it to its best.

A significant part of the larder that Gille had ordered for the feast had been replenished in a single day. Meat would be gorged on over the next few days, then dried, cured and salted for the leaner days when the hunting brought only rabbits, grouse and ptarmigan. I couldn't recall a day in the field as successful as this.

The two leaders dismounted, Macbeth still with a spring in his legs, Gille more laboured. They clapped their arms round each other's shoulders and stumbled towards us. I could smell the sweat and the ale while they were still a few strides from us. 'Our cousin is quite the hunter,' Gille shouted, a slur in his voice. 'A mad, reckless fool, but a lucky one too.' He prodded Macbeth in the ribs. 'I was sure that big bastard boar would have you on its tusks.' Back to me. 'But our fancy-dancer cousin skipped away and sliced the life from it as it bolted past.'

Macbeth grinned like a small boy who's caught the biggest pike in the pond. 'Not lucky, Gille. Possessed of perfect judgement.'

Gille snorted. 'Aye, you keep thinking that, Deircc. We'll see who survives longest, the lucky or the canny.' He reached for me and crushed me to his chest, planting a slobbery kiss on my cheek.

I thought I was the only one who heard the threat lying under those words till I caught a sudden wariness in Macbeth's eyes.

Gille let me go and turned to face our people, who had swiftly materialised from homes and workplaces at the arrival of the hunters. 'You are the fortunate ones,' he declaimed. 'You're the clan of Gille Coemgáin, the well-bred and the well-fed of Moray. Tonight, we will eat well, thanks to my prowess in the hunt.'

They cheered. Of course, they did. They knew only too well which side of the bed was the comfortable one. The hunters dispersed, their arms around each other, Macbeth's men already best of friends with the Mormaer's boys. They'd be drinking horn for horn as soon as they'd stripped off their hunting leathers. By the time the food arrived, they'd stuff themselves without tasting a morsel. But they'd be happy, satisfied with their manly accomplishments. I turned to Ligach and said softly, 'Tell our women to keep their distance. I don't want the visitors thinking they can help themselves to everything under the Mormaer's wing.'

She nodded and moved away on her mission.

'Eithne, talk to the cooks, see what they need from you to prepare and preserve this mountain of meat. Aife, with me.' I led the way back to our quarters. I wanted it noted where I went and with whom.

'What is it you need from me?' Aife asked as soon as we were alone.

'I need to meet with Macbeth. In secret. Nobody must know. I mean that, Aife. Our lives depend on it.'

Her smile was knowing. 'You have a plan.'

'The very bare beginnings of a plan.'

'Eithne swears she has a love potion.'

'She only swears that to fools who have coin in their purse. I have no need of Eithne here. I know well enough how to make a man loose his restraints and beg, against *all his judgement. So where is the place for such a meeting?'*

She sat down and cupped her chin in her hands. She spoke slowly, thinking out loud. I did not interrupt. 'It must be within the palisade. Darkling, out of the glow of the torches . . . Behind the stables, where Beorth keeps the horses' saddles and bridles? Not before the meal, though; Beorth will still be busy after the hunt. Not during the meal either, for Gille will keep a close watch on Macbeth. And he always keeps a watch on you . . .' She frowned and sighed. 'He never wants you after feasting, does he?'

I shook my head. 'No. The one time he did, his prick lay shrivelled like a pickled carrot. I tried. All the tricks I've heard the women blether about. But nothing worked. He raged at me, called me every kind of beldam under the moon. He blamed me to my face, but since that time, he's never ordered me to him after feasting.'

'So he has no eyes on you after the feasting is over and we retire to our rooms?'

I nodded. 'But his men watch me.'

Aife closed her eyes and considered. She thinks like a hawk; when she considers a place, it's as if she can see it mapped out before her as a bird of prey would. Every dwelling, every workshop, the great hall, the passages that run among them, every way in and out of the courtyard. Macbeth's men are camped between the

palisade and the backside of the great hall, that much I
did know. But the details were a mystery to me.

At length she opened her eyes and fixed her steady
grey gaze on mine. 'Macbeth is lodged on the opposite
side of the great hall to Gille?'

I nodded. 'Where all honoured guests lie.'

'But there would be nothing suspicious if he went
among his own men after the feasting?'

I shrugged. 'It would be natural enough.'

'If he walked out wearing a bunnet over his hair and a
cloak . . .' Thinking out loud. 'And if a man wearing the
cloak and bunnet returned to his lodging a few minutes
later, the watchers would believe it was Macbeth
returning?'

'I suppose so . . .' I began to grasp where Aife was
heading.

'Macbeth could cut through his men's tents, round
behind the stables and make his way to Beorth's tack room.'

'So he could. But Aife, how am I supposed to get
there?'

A deep sigh. 'You think Gille's men still watch our
door after we have come to bed?'

'I know they do. Gille is a man steeped in suspicion,
you know that.'

Aife growls in the back of her throat, then gets up and
goes to the window at the rear of our outer chamber. It's
too high for her to see out of, but she pulls a stool

towards her, brushes the curtain to one side and peers out into the darkness. There are no buildings between us and the palisade; we are at the rear of the compound, and to get behind us an enemy would have to fight their way past everyone else. 'So he comes to you,' she said without a quaver in her voice. 'We drop a stool down to him and he climbs in.' She turned back and stepped lightly down. 'That would work.'

I felt a sudden overwhelming doubt, a physical lurch in my guts. 'What if he doesn't want to take the risk?'

She scoffed. 'Of course, he'll take the risk. How can you doubt that? I've seen the way he looks at you when he thinks Gille's eyes are elsewhere.'

'And where will you be? You and Eithne and Ligach?'

A one-shouldered shrug. 'Well, you know how Gille loves those honey cakes I make? We'll be baking honey cakes as a breakfast surprise for Gille and his guests.'

'In the middle of the night?'

Her smile was the very model of mischief. 'The baker will love us for lifting some of his burden.'

Even as I turn, I register it's no monk. With no time to plan, I reach for the dagger at my waist, its handle towards my hand. Without hesitation, I plunge it into the chest of the man at the door. He cries out. Falls against me. I pull away and there is blood everywhere. My hands, scarlet. Ligach is at my side, Aife too. Angus pushes my victim to the floor.

'It's the Seaton boy,' he whispers, his face ashen grey. 'The turncoat Seaton boy.'

The Seaton boy – for this moment has stripped his manhood from him – gasps like a landed fish. The colour is draining from his face as the blood pumps from his chest. None of us moves to help him. We all know inevitable death when we see it.

I let the dagger fall to the floor and step away. But Aife is ahead of me. She steers me to the washbasin and pours out fresh water. 'Wash your hands,' she tells me. I obey; it doesn't cross my mind to do otherwise. I'm a woman hexed, shocked and locked by my actions.

Slowly, dimly, I become aware of what's happening around me. I see Angus picking up my dagger and laying it next to Brother Brendan. Ligach is making neat packs of our clothes, tying them with cords. Eithne is fastening leather straps round her medicine chest. I know what comes next, and I do not want it.

Angus crosses the room and pats my hands dry with a rough piece of linen. 'My brave queen, it's time.' His voice is gentle but firm. I cannot speak but I nod my understanding. He turns away and begins packing what food we have into a coarse sack. Aife takes me back to our inner chamber and strips me of my blood-soaked clothes, then dresses me in my warmest woollen gown and a heavy cloak that does not look in the least regal. She bundles my ruined clothes together and stuffs them into a leather game bag.

She brings me a cup of mead and holds me close while I drink it. By the time I'm finished, I'm beginning to feel more capable of playing the queen. I get to my feet and when I emerge in our barn, I see the others are also dressed for the open air of March, with its spirited winds and shrouds of mist.

The women shoulder their burdens and Angus hoists Eithne's box on his back. In silence, we creep out of the barn. The monastery is in darkness, but there's a glimmer of light from the waning moon, enough to guide our feet along a well-known path. We take the route through the vegetable beds that leads to the short crossing to the lochside. It's sheltered from the wind; we will be across in a matter of minutes.

The monastery boats are hauled up on the sand. Angus chooses a low wooden punt and pushes it to the water's edge. He loads our burdens, then hands us aboard. He grunts with the effort of getting us under way, but he's a strong man and we're soon bobbing across the narrow strait.

There's a jolt as we hit the far shore, then we're moving again. We hurry up the beach into the shelter of a narrow path through the whin bushes. When we're about to run out of cover, Angus holds up a hand to still us. 'Wait here,' he says in a low voice.

We hunker down in the lee of the bushes and wait. 'Why did Angus leave my dagger behind? I have no protection now.' That seems the most important thing to me now.

'It will look as if Brendan is the man who killed Seaton,' Ligach explains, her voice softer than it usually is when she's explaining what seems obvious to her but obscure to the rest of us. 'Either Brendan will be awake, bewildered and with no memory of anything, or he will still be deep in his drugged dreams, in which case, Malcolm's other spy will assume he stabbed the Seaton lad, then drank himself insensible in remorse.'

'And the monks will not betray us,' Aife adds. 'Either way, there will be no report back to Malcolm of our presence.'

'But what about Brendan? He'll be blamed. He might even be killed himself.' Eithne covers her mouth with her hand, aghast.

'More blood on my hands,' I moan softly.

'No, Gruoch. Brendan will not be executed. The abbot will understand the truth,' Ligach says, confident as ever. 'Malcolm's man will leave as soon as he can. Just as soon as he's decided whether to carry on alone to Abernethy or to report back directly to his lord. The abbot will assure him that Brendan will face the penalty for his crime, but he'll find a reason to wait until the spy has gone.'

I look into her face, seeking reassurance and finding it. 'Thank you, Ligach.' Then we all notice Eithne has started rocking gently back and forth. We all know what this means and there's no postponing it or avoiding it.

Aife strokes her back, making quiet soothing noises. When Eithne speaks, it's a gentle mumble. 'To the west,' she repeats half a dozen times. 'Across the sea, to the west.'

'To Mull?' Aife prompts gently. 'The land of Macbeth?'

'To the west, beyond,' Eithne says. 'All the way west. All the way.' She mutters the same thing several times, then slumps against Aife.

'Well, that seems clear enough,' Ligach says drily. 'For once.'

We all subside into silence. I still feel stunned, as if I'd breathed in too much of one of Eithne's herbs. Nothing feels real. I can't make sense of myself. I have killed a man and must flee to who knows where, who knows what. I once had a husband, a son, a kingdom. All gone now. I'm like the monastery boat. Unmoored, cast on a strange shore, adrift with grief.

How do I live now?

The feast felt interminable. The women brought out
platters of meat, bread cakes slathered in butter, mounds

of roasted carrots and apples. Macbeth laughed at the
amount of food that appeared. 'Cousin,' he exclaimed.
'I thought you emptied the larders in our honour last
night. But I see now how much you were holding back.
Had you a more honoured guest in mind?'

We all laughed, some of us more nervously than
others. But Gille appeared not to be offended. 'We kept
some back,' he said. 'We knew you'd feel so well
harboured that you'd be reluctant to return home.'

'With hunting like this on the doorstep, we may
never leave.' Macbeth raised his cup of ale and toasted
the room. His eyes met mine momentarily in what felt
like a promise. I couldn't understand how that link
between us had been forged so swiftly, so suddenly. Yet I
couldn't deny its existence.

I was no foolish virgin, waiting for a hero to rescue
me. But in Macbeth, I saw a possibility I'd barely been
able to consider before. It was a route so perilous I
wondered at my even imagining it. But at the end of
those risks might lie safety for me and the three women
whose love had sustained me through every threat and
difficulty. Out of the nettle of danger, I might close my
hand tight and pluck the flower of safety.

So I made sure my eyes never strayed towards him for
the rest of the meal. I reserved my smiles for Gille,
laughing at his jests and praising his skills at the hunt. The
toasts went round and round, every man determined not

to be outdone when it came to flattering his lord. Through it all, I was proud to see my women enthuse with the rest of the room, as if they were loyal as Gille's bodyguard.

The feasting seemed to last forever. Knowing I had to remain visible to Gille made the grains of sand in the hourglass in my head run even more slow. But finally, Gille drained his last draught of barley bree and stood, swaying slightly. 'If we are to hunt tomorrow, we must rest tonight,' he announced, tripping almost imperceptibly over his t's. To the practised eye, it was clear he was very drunk. His body servant stood discreetly at his elbow, braced for the arm that would be slung over his shoulders. It looked like comradeship, but I knew it for dependency.

'Goodnight, husband,' I said, managing a warm smile. 'Sleep well and rise rested.'

He leered at me. 'You can depend on that, wife.' I suppressed a shudder at the veiled promise. There was a brief lull as he made his unsteady way from the hall, but as soon as he had gone, those who were still capable of drinking more did just that. I nodded to the women, and we left together, making our way through the rabble to our quarters.

As we closed the door behind us, Ligach said, 'I've told the servers, no more barrels should be broached. It's time for them all to bed down for the night.'

'And Macbeth? Is he ready?'

'I saw he had a cut on his arm, badly bandaged,'
Eithne said. *'So Aife and I went to his quarters before the feast. I cleaned the wound, put ointment and a clean dressing on it.'*

Aife picked up the tale. *'I spoke to him out of the hearing of his men. I told him you sought a private audience with him.'*

Eithne again. *'He stopped noticing the pain from his arm.'* She giggled.

'He asked how that would be possible and I outlined the plan. We could see how eager he is to see you by his failure to question it.'

My heart quickened with excitement. I understood the risks; of course, I did. If we were to be found out, we would all die – me, Aife, Eithne, Ligach. And Macbeth himself. Nevertheless, the prospect of the time ahead thrilled me with delighted anticipation. Perhaps the fear made the idea of the encounter all the more tantalising? If that were true, perhaps we should always try to salt our dalliances with a little danger.

'We must prepare you,' Eithne said.

'I know what lies ahead,' I said, perhaps a little too sharp.

'It's not just the act that matters, it's the atmosphere.'
This, from Ligach, the most practical of my three companions, came as a surprise. We all knew about her

*liaison with Angus, the man assigned by Gille to protect
and serve us, but if I gave it any thought at all, I imagined
her bedding him as a brisk and transactional matter. I
wasn't sure how comfortable I was with the idea of a
romantic element to their relationship. I have never
trusted divided loyalties; when choices have to be made,
they can more easily come down on the wrong side.*

*As if she sensed my unease, she patted my arm. 'Do
not think I would ever put Angus above you, my queen.
I do not play at dice with our lives. My body serves to
keep Angus closer to us than to your husband. He is far
more in thrall to me than I to him.' She smiles, slow and
sensual. 'That it's also a pleasure is a gift.'*

*Even as she spoke, Aife was removing my clothes.
Eithne brought a basin of warm water perfumed with
rose and whin blossom, and I stood naked and obedient
as she bathed me from head to foot. Once I was dried,
Aife replaced my heavy formal garments with a light
linen shift that fell below my knees. She assessed me,
hands on hips and muttered, 'Something with the hair.'*

*She unpinned the careful plaiting and coiling of my
hair and let it flow over my shoulders in loose waves.
'That's it,' Ligach said. 'You look like the queen of the
bedchamber, my lady.'*

*Aife shooed me towards the door. 'Now away into
your sleeping quarters, Gruoch. We'll see Macbeth safely
in, then we'll take ourselves off to the bakery to make*

the honey cakes like good little body servants.' The three
of them shared the kind of secret smile that women
understand.

I went through to my bedchamber and arranged myself
on the settle. I'd done this often enough for Gille's benefit,
to speed things to their conclusion. But for the first time I
was making it a willing seduction. I wanted there to be no
time for second thoughts for either of us, but I didn't want
to display myself on the bed like a whore.

My heart was racing, and I was in the shivery grip of
suspense at the prospect of Macbeth's body against mine.
I had been traded to a man for advantage once before;
this time, if things ran the way I planned, I might take
charge of such a trade. Minutes passed with agonising
slowness for the second time that night. At last I heard
the low murmur of voices followed by a muffled scuffle
and the sound of boots landing on rushes. Moments later,
I heard the outer door to our quarters close, then the
rustle of footsteps approaching.

The time for turning back was gone.

I perch on one of the bundles of clothes in a dwam, waiting
for Angus with no sense of how much time is passing. At
some point, Aife disappears down a virtually invisible track

through the prickles of the whin bushes. When she returns, the game bag flops against her hip, empty. Ligach looks a question at her. 'Buried in the sand among the bushes,' Aife says.

If Malcolm's remaining man thinks to search the barn, he'll find no trace of us. Since we had to flee after we lost the battle at Dunsinane, we've behaved as if we might have to run at any time. We live as simply as possible; most of my formal robes are in a big press by the abbot's rooms. Aife collects them when I need to present the image of a queen and returns them afterwards. What we keep in our quarters are no more than we need in the day-to-day. And we can strip that out in no time.

I wish we could see St Serf's Isle from our hiding place, to have a sense of what is going on. How much grace do we have before Malcolm's man starts to doubt the tale we've presented him with? And what then? Will his instinct be to flee, perhaps across the very stretch of water that stands between us and the monastery isle? Or will he head back the way he came, back north to report this disaster to Malcolm?

I know what I'd choose if I were in his boots. It wouldn't be going back empty-handed to Malcolm. Not if I wanted to live.

I can't help wondering about poor bewildered Brendan. It's easier than thinking about having killed a man. Brendan will surface from his strange dreams into a stranger reality. Will he believe he used the dagger to end a man's life? Will he think we were part of his dream, that we never actually existed? But then he'll look out at the hives and remember the hours spent with Eithne and the bees. Another man would have the consolation of his beliefs. It's called an 'order' for a reason; it has an iron routine that leaves no room for doubt. But Brendan lives by his doubt, and this will be hard for him.

I feel more sorry for Brendan than I do for the Seaton boy.

Ligach digs into the inner pocket of her cloak and produces two apples. She takes out her knife and cuts them in half. The moonlight catches the sharp edge and I shudder. I scold myself in my head; I cannot go through life starting in horror every time someone produces a blade. That way madness lies.

I accept my share of the apple and nibble at its edges. I have no appetite but I know that the way ahead will be long, dangerous and uncertain. To refuse food when it is offered is a false heroism.

The cry of an owl cuts through the night. Angus, at last. He creeps into our refuge, and behind him I see the means of escape we planned mere days after we arrived here almost four years ago. We emerge from the bushes on to rough pasture. Four sturdy ponies and a pack horse with a slipe attached to its harness await. The two broad planks of the slipe will be space enough for what we have brought with us, the lattices on the sides and the back enough to hold our baggage securely once we have fastened the straps.

We load the slipe, and Angus turns to me, his hand inside his jerkin. 'Not yours, my queen, but almost as good.' He hands me a dagger. He's lying; it's even better than mine, perfectly balanced in the hand. I test the blade against my thumb and nod my approval. 'I sharpened it myself,' he assures me.

I'm not sure I'm ready for such a gift, but to proceed without it would be irresponsible. He looks expectant and I squeeze his arm. 'You're a good man, Angus. I'm glad we've got you with us.'

Glowing with praise, he mounts the packhorse, his legs barely straddling its broad back.

We four each take the nearest pony. I find myself aboard a skittish roan, whose mood suits me well. To my astonishment, there is an arbalest in a kind of holster attached to one side of the saddle. On the other side, a quiver of sturdy bolts for it. I've never used one of these crossbows, but I've seen their power in battle. Their brutal force makes hunting bows look like toys. I turn to Angus. 'Shouldn't you have the arbalest?'

He shakes his head. 'If we come under attack, you need to take cover while we take on the attackers. You're the prize here, my queen. You can use the arbalest to best effect from cover, trust me.'

I exchange looks with my women. They nod their heads in agreement. I see they're each equipped with sturdy hunting bows and arrows. We look capable, and that's half the battle.

We form up: Aife and Ligach in front, Angus in the middle, Eithne and me bringing up the rear. It's not ideal; separating Aife and Eithne is never the best policy. Ligach and I are the most experienced hunters so we'd do best in front; but I am the valuable cargo and so I must be protected. Ideally, I'd be in the middle, but we decided when we first drew up this plan that I could not ride the pack horse in comfort.

And so we set off, the moon setting behind us, the darkness cloaking us. We have grown to feel safe on the isle; the question is whether our instincts are still sharp enough to keep us alive to journey's end.

The door curtain shifted to one side, and the candles flickered. Macbeth stood outlined in the light, his red hair reflecting the glow as if lit from within. Something shifted inside me. 'My lady,' he said softly. He looked around warily, scouring the shadows for danger. 'Your women summoned me.'

I smiled my reassurance. 'This is no trick. You are safe here. You have my word.'

He stayed in the doorway, his eyes shifting to meet mine. 'They said you wanted to see me.'

'More than see you.' My voice surprised me, husky

*with a desire I'd never felt for my husband. At that
moment, I forgot this was a stratagem and let my body
take charge.*

He crossed the floor and gestured at the settle. 'May I?'

*In response, I reached for his hand and pulled him
down beside me. I felt a wave of heat from his body; if I
had been ice, I would have melted, but I am flesh and
blood and I was drawn irresistibly to that warmth. Where
our bodies touched it was like a lick of flame running
through me. 'You have been my mind's constant
companion since last night.' It was a bold statement for
any woman to have made, but even more so for a woman
in my position. I knew the risk but I no longer cared.
This was my one chance, and I could not let it go by me.*

*The creases round his eyes deepened as he smiled.
'All day in the saddle, I could not stop thinking of you.
I feared I'd perform like a callow youth in the hunt, but
I think you must have spurred me on to greater things.'
He leaned forward and chastely kissed my forehead, his
lips firm and dry against my skin.*

*After that, there was little need for words. Our
bodies knew what our hearts desired. Our clothes
puddled on the floor, our bodies tangled on the bed,
hands and mouths exploring new territories, hard muscle
against soft flesh, then the overwhelm of union. We were
lost to the world, deep in discovery, searching for even
more satisfaction.*

At last, exhausted, we pulled the furs over us and lay wrapped around each other as comfortably as if we'd been partnered for years, not scant hours. Finally, I understood what the act could mean. The more we'd loved, the more my appetite for him grew, as if it fed on itself.

It was a world away from Gille's idea of congress. I dared hope that the wisp of an idea that had underpinned this encounter might work. 'I want this forever,' I said.

He kissed me. 'I wish your father had set his sights on me, not my cousin.'

'But we will be together again?' I hoped he heard the plea in my voice.

'We will find a way, be sure of that.'

'Tomorrow? Again?'

He held me close, and I felt his prick harden against me once more. 'What's wrong with now?'

And it began again, that contrapunto of flesh and frenzy. Afterwards, we ended up side by side, sweating and panting.

'I must leave for Mull at first light,' he said.

'No!' I exclaimed, turning to cover his body with mine. 'Not now we have discovered this.'

His face contorted in despair. 'I cannot stay in your orbit and act normally. I'm not good enough at putting on a false face And you? I look at you and I see you're glowing. Gille will see that too. He may be a brute but he's not a fool. The risk is too great.'

My heart rebelled, but my head knew he was right.

This madness had not been my plan. I wanted only to bewitch him so I could preserve my place. We'd fucked like animals for a night; perhaps Macbeth's potent seed would take root in my womb. A child would appease Gille and secure my position. A boy would make me valuable; if it were a girl, I could go a second bout with our beautiful cousin.

Rescue had been my stratagem, one way or another. I had not counted on this revelation. I had not anticipated the tidal surge of emotion.

I had not known love so I had not expected it.

The horses' hooves find tracks that elude our dark-blind eyes. They walk steadily and only hesitate when paths diverge. Thankfully it's a clear night and Angus knows how to navigate by the stars, so we soon learn to steer our mounts in the direction that best suits our destination.

'Where are we headed?' Ligach asks once we're well under way and as sure as we can be that there's no pursuit.

'Mull is a safe haven for us,' I say. 'When Macbeth was their lord, they loved him. They'll honour us.'

'Or at least leave us be,' Ligach mutters.

'Mull? The island?' Aife sounds incredulous. 'How do we get to Mull?'

'We ride for four or five days,' Angus says. 'We're aiming for Dun Ollaigh fort. It's one of the seats of the kings of Dál Riata.'

'Dál Riata? Are they still our friends?' Eithne asks, vague as ever in matters of high politics.

'Back in the day, Kenneth MacAlpin built strong bonds with them. They honoured him. Since I'm a direct descendant of the High King MacAlpin, like Macbeth was, they'll treat us with respect. They'll not betray us, even if they've heard about Lulach's death and our flight. We can send to Mull for a boat then.' I try to sound reassuring.

I sense unease from Eithne alongside me. 'How will we be safe for four or five days?' she asks in a low voice. 'We have no way of knowing who our friends are.'

'We'll travel by night and find places to rest during the day. We have some food, and there are fish in the streams and rabbits on the hills. We'll stay away from people. We'll be fine, Eithne.'

There's a stubborn set to her mouth. I know she doesn't believe me. I'm not sure I even believe myself, but there's no alternative. It's been years since I travelled to Mull, and I remember it being a hard road back then. A dozen years on my bones won't have made it any easier.

Dawn comes up behind us and it's soon joined by a gusty wind from the north-east. The horses whicker as it swirls round their fetlocks and tousles their manes. We're in the foothills of small mountains now, not the wild summits of the far north, but still it's harder going for our mounts.

Eithne is giving me a lesson in the plants we're passing. I know she's trying to lift her own spirits but also stir me back to myself and the days before Macbeth and I wed, and I'm grateful for it. 'Can you smell the ramsons?' she asks, pointing to a carpet of leaves shaped like tall shields, wee white flowers waving among them. 'You know that smell, that taste?'

It's unmistakable. 'Wild garlic. You make a paste with it for the cooks, for flavouring stews and meat.' I pull a face. 'You're making me hungry just thinking about it.'

She chuckles. 'It's good for the blood. See they wee yellow flowers? They're called pilewort. They've got knobbly bundles of roots. Can you guess what I use them for? The clue's in the name, and the shape of the roots?'

Now it's my turn to laugh. 'Would that be piles?'

'Well worked out, Gruoch. I love this time of year, when the flowers start to keek out in the woodlands and the hillsides. Milk-gowans, wood anemone, dog's mercury, primroses. They're bonny, and they're useful. All kinds of medicines and ointments and dyes for our cloth. And for the pot too. Nettle soup and milk-gowan salad.'

Eithne's trick is working. I'm starting to pay attention to my surroundings now, coming back to myself. 'And the trees. The blackthorn and the rowan, they're coming into leaf.'

'The year's turning towards summer. We're coming into the light, leaving the darkness behind. All will be well, for all of us.'

I'm not so sure about that but I can't help loving Eithne's optimism. Considering the things she sees in her visions, it's nothing short of miraculous.

We turn into a shallow glen and come up against the first habitation we've seen since we left in the dark. A couple of small huts, a pen for goats, half a dozen scrabbling chickens and a thin trickle of peat smoke emerging from a hole in one thatched roof. Two young children are playing with a bundle of chicken feathers in the dirt. As soon as they see us, they scream and run inside.

As we approach, a woman emerges, a man at her back. They look astonished, as if they can't quite believe there's anyone else in the world. Ligach reins her horse in, and we all come to a halt. 'Good day,' Ligach says. They look blank. She tries Pictish; it's still spoken where there's little contact with the rest of the country.

The man replies. I dredge my memory of the old tongue and understand he's asking where we're bound. Ligach lies. Something about 'druimean'. I'm not sure if it's a place name or just a landscape feature. Ligach cheerily tells them we're on our way to her sister's wedding. It seems to satisfy the man, who says something else I don't catch. We all raise a hand in farewell and carry on.

'What was that he said at the end?' I ask.

'There's a small band of raiders in the next glen, but I lied about where we're going – that's not on our route. We'll be fine.'

I can feel my horse is growing tired. 'We need to find somewhere to rest soon, Angus. The horses are weary, and so am I.'

'Aye.' I can see he's scouring the hillside, looking for shelter and grazing. Up ahead, there's a patch of woodland near the track. Behind it, a little further up the slope, there's a clearing. Angus catches sight of it at the same time as I do. We both point and say, 'Over there.'

We turn off the track and head for the shelter. It's a struggle for the slipe, and a couple of times I fear the heavy horse will lose its footing. But it's dogged, and with Angus's encouragement we make it to the shelter of the trees.

It's a relief to get back on my own two feet. Even at a walking pace, riding is an effort, and I've not had any long days on horseback since we moved to the isle. Muscles I'd forgotten about were stiff and sore, and I wasn't the only one swearing as we tethered our mounts in reach of the coarse moorland grasses.

We agreed that Angus should take the first watch with Aife and Eithne. Ligach and I curl up together under the trees with a couple of wolfskins for warmth. I say warmth, but really all they're good for is to keep the wind out. In spite of the cold, I fall asleep as soon as I pillow my head on my forearm.

When Angus shakes me awake, the sun is past its midpoint. He settles down between Aife and Eithne, who treat him as a human cushion. By the time Ligach and I have crouched in the bushes to empty our bladders, he's snoring. Ligach stations herself at one end of the clearing behind a boulder, the arbalest resting on it; if trouble is going to come, that's the likely direction.

The dray horse is lying down, gentle breathing making its stomach rise and fall. I sit down, leaning against it, smelling its sweet breath, an arrow nocked on my bowstring. I watch a pair of eagles dancing above the hill, chasing each other, breaking off to swoop dramatically away, then stooping for prey. It's hypnotic, but not so much so that I forget the sharp sorrow in my heart. Nor to pay attention.

Just as well. A movement strikes the corner of my eye, and at the far end of the trees I catch the shape of a man. 'Ligach!' I shout. 'Over here!'

I'm thankful that she still possesses a turn of speed that's beyond most men. She is by my side in seconds, just as the figure in the trees breaks out into the open. My cry has warned him there's no further point in stealth, and he runs towards us, followed by two others, all brandishing claymores and shouting the battle cries that are meant to strike fear into our hearts.

'Oh shit!' Ligach cries, taking aim with the arbalest.

The bolt strikes the first bandit in the throat, and he falls like a stone. While she's reloading her weapon, I line up a shot at one of the others but my arrow whistles past him. Thankfully Angus is already at my side, woken by the clamour. He looses off an arrow, catching one of the attackers in the thigh. He collapses to one knee, trying to free the arrow, not realising the peaceful monks' armourer favours barbed tips.

As Ligach fires again, hitting the wounded man in the chest, I realise Aife has circled behind them and shot the third man in the back. His momentum drives him on to his stomach in time for Eithne to run from the trees, screaming like a banshee, waving her knife, and slicing deep into his neck. She knows where to strike, no one better; blood jets in a fountain from his neck and she has to jump clear to prevent it splashing her.

Two dead and one wounded. Not bad for a quartet of women and one man. Angus grabs the claymore of the one Ligach killed outright and approaches the third man. He's clearly mortally wounded, but I don't think he knows that yet. He waves his claymore feebly and Angus kicks it to one side. 'Are there more of you?' he demands.

'Next glen,' comes out in a defiant gurgle.

'How many?' This is Ligach.

He gives her a look of vicious hatred, and who could blame him? 'Enough to . . . fucking finish you . . . bitch.'

Coolly, she stamps on his wounded leg. He screams in

agony, a very different sound from his battle cry. 'How many?' she snarls.

He moans. 'Seven.'

We exchange looks. Time to move, without delay. Angus takes out his knife and cuts the man's throat in one swift slice. Not, I suspect, out of kindness, but rather to make sure there's nobody left to tell the tale of four mad women and a single man, all capable of slaughter. In a few short minutes, I have ceased to be the only killer among us.

I am not ashamed to say I was glad of the company.

Macbeth was as good as his word. Come the morning, he announced to all in the hall that in spite of the delights of our hospitality he and his men would return to his steading on Mull. 'I would not stand upon the order of my going, my lord Gille Coemgáin,' he said. 'I'll go at once, while I'm still welcome at your table.'

'We're sorry to see you leave, cousin. Haste ye back!' Gille managed to sound sincere, but I doubted he was. He liked to be acknowledged best at everything. But everybody had seen that Macbeth was a better huntsman and a better dancer. Gille hated to be outshone; had he known Macbeth was also an infinitely better lover, his cousin would never have made it back to Mull alive.

Nevertheless they clapped each other on the back, apparently the best of friends as well as kinsmen. We women watched from the benches outside our quarters as they saddled up and trotted out in tight formation. Macbeth cast not one look in my direction, and I was glad, for I would as lief not struggle to maintain my composure. My body ached sweetly and that was enough.

It seemed absurd after such a short acquaintance, but I missed him every day. The sound of his voice in private moments; the weight of his body on mine; the smoky smell of his hair; the feel of his skin – all this and more, I ached for. I made sure that I was compelled to Gille's bedchamber soon after Macbeth and his men had left, to cover myself should the outcome be what I'd settled for. But I built a wall around myself more even than before. I didn't want the memories of Macbeth to be tainted by the reality of my husband.

Of course, Gille noticed nothing.

It was Eithne who saw the change in me. I was aware that she was watching me more closely than usual; she had started to prepare different concoctions for my evening drink, herbs and spices in combinations I'd not had before. When I questioned her, she simply said, 'You need to keep your strength up.' For what, she didn't say.

And then almost three weeks after Macbeth had visited me, I understood the reason. My monthly courses had not appeared. I had always been irregular on occasion so I hadn't realised immediately. But Eithne knew without counting. She sat me down with Aife and Ligach in our quarters one morning after we had broken our fast. I'd been particularly hungry, demanding eggs and bannocks washed down with small ale.

'You have an appetite,' she began.

'We all do sometimes,' I said, a little puzzled at why she'd mentioned it.

'But we're not all with child.'

I stared at her, not quite believing her. 'How do you know?'

Eithne shrugged. 'I just do.'

'Your courses are late,' Ligach pointed out. 'And you are eating like a horse that's been ridden hard.'

Aife smirked. 'Oh, I think we all know she's been ridden hard.' They all titter like smutty children. 'Your plan has worked, Gruoch. Macbeth has succeeded where Gille failed.'

I wanted to believe them. But I also understood the enormity of it. The feelings Macbeth had provoked in my heart had undermined my goal. I yearned for him; I was revolted by Gille's touch. The idea of raising Macbeth's child under Gille's roof, as Gille's bairn, made me feel sick. The fall-back plan I'd considered so clever had turned into a terrible trap.

And I had no idea how to escape it.

❦

We pause only to drag the bodies under the cover of the trees, then we pack up and set off again. We soon reach the end of the glen, where the track splits in two. To the south-west, the trail is wider and smoother, but we can see in the distance a threatening column of smoke. 'That'll be the rest of the raiders,' Ligach observes. 'I take it we head in the other direction?'

'Aye,' Angus says. 'We'll be among the trees in no time. We'll have to go in single file, though. The path is too narrow for you to ride in pairs.'

So Ligach leads off, me at her back. Then Aife, Eithne and Angus in the rear. Although the path is narrow, it seems well-trodden, the beaten earth hard beneath the horses' hooves. The air smells soft and fresh, the scent of new growth all around us. There's a burn to one side of the trail, and the sound of its burbling mingles with the calls of small birds as we make our way up the glen. We're even sheltered from the wind by dense woodland on either side.

On any other day, it would have been a pleasure. But the knowledge that we are hunted cuts through everything. Whenever we stop to relieve ourselves or just to stretch our legs, I sense the same tension in all of us. As darkness falls, we can see the woodland thinning out and beyond that, a cluster of buildings. Not a compound but a substantial enough group to be considered a danger.

We come alongside each other on the edge of the wood. 'I think this place is called Crubha,' Angus says. 'They trade cattle here. The roads cross here from the north and from Fife.'

'Is it safe?' I ask.

'Nowhere is safe,' Ligach says. 'Can we pass it by?'

'I think if we follow the western course of the river, we should manage not to attract much attention.' Angus looks less certain than he sounds.

'I'll go ahead to scout the route,' Aife volunteers.

Eithne demurs and Ligach tries to take her place, but Angus insists she stay. 'You're the bonniest fechter,' he says. 'And Aife looks harmless.'

Aife chuckles. 'Sometimes it's useful to look harmless.' Without further argument, she trots off. Waiting is no less trying than the night before, but at least we're further away from pursuit. The horses champ the grasses and Ligach cuts slices from a ham we'd had in the barn. I chew the meat slowly, remembering the adage that hunger is the best sauce.

By the time Aife returns, we're all too much on edge even to speak to each other. 'We can do it,' she announces. 'The only possible problem is a burn that goes off to the side of the river. But there's a ford, and it barely covered my hooves. I think the slipe will make it.'

She's almost right. We're nearly across when the heavy horse stumbles. The slipe's load shifts, and for a terrible moment, it looks as if we might lose it all, until Angus jumps off and pulls on the horse's harness to help it right itself. Our supplies survive. But Angus is wet and cold now; I insist we stop for him to put on dry clothes. There are some quiet murmurs of dissent, but Eithne speaks up. 'We need Angus. We won't make it if he falls ill with a fever.'

There's no shelter here, just waist-high reeds, but Angus is swift. He strips off his wet clothes and dresses in whatever comes to hand. They're not as warm but they'll have to do till the others dry out. At last we're on our way again.

The track widens once more and it's mostly flat, so we make good progress. We pass through a village with no sign of life; not even the sound of our hooves rouses anyone to come to the door of their hovel. I feel more secure now we've managed to negotiate two settlements without a problem.

'We're in the lands where the Picts and Scots came together,' Angus said. 'Your descent from Kenneth MacAlpin carries weight in these parts. They will feel more kindly disposed towards us than towards Malcolm.' It's a comforting thought and I recite the line of descent in my head to the rhythm of my mount's steps.

The moon puts in an appearance again when we reach

the place where the river emerges from a loch. It illuminates an extraordinary sight. A single dilapidated wooden structure at the end of a long pier jutting out into the loch like a man-made island. It's too big and too solid to be a fishing hut. 'Do people live here?' I ask.

'They used to,' Angus says. 'Back in the olden days.'

On another day, I'd be eager to explore. But there's no time for that, and besides, even kissed by moonlight, the pier doesn't look very safe. If nothing else, this flight is revealing my country to me. How empty it is, how beautiful in its starkness. I wish Macbeth was with me; he could tell me so much more than even Angus knows.

On we press, along a shore that seems to go on forever. Dawn is breaking and we're still not quite at the end of the loch, though we can almost make it out as the darkness lifts. There are trees to the right of us, and we manage to find a way through them to a clearing. Gratefully, we dismount and settle down for the night. We agree that only one person need keep watch; there has been no sign of life for miles.

I stretch my stiff muscles and settle into the familiar congruence of limbs I've shared with my women over the years. As I drift into sleep, I almost forget we're fugitives. It's a blessing I won't be able to hold on to for much longer.

*I waited for another month to pass before I revealed my
pregnancy to Gille Coemgáin. I wanted to put time and
space between Macbeth's visit and my state so as to allay
any suspicions my husband might entertain. I didn't suffer
from morning sickness, thanks either to my own
constitution or, if you believe Eithne, to the quantities of
ginger and peppermint tea she plied me with at every
opportunity. Either way, it helped the deception.*

*I managed to hold my tongue until I was summoned
to his chamber. When he laid hands on me, I backed
away. 'My lord, you must not!' He stopped in his tracks,
astonished at my temerity. 'I am with child,' I said
simply, my face wreathed in smiles.*

*'You're carrying my child?' Pure delight lit up his
eyes and a slow grin spread across his lips. I almost felt a
moment's guilt. Almost. He seized my hands and kissed
me with enough force to split my lip. 'But this is glorious
news. We must have a feast!' He pulled me to him, but
I wriggled free.*

*'No, my lord Gille! You must not crush me so. It has
taken so long for this to happen, we must take no chances
with my precious burden. I could not bear it if our
carelessness caused . . .' I manage to sound piteous.*

*He jumps back as if I'd prodded him with a hot fire
iron. 'Forgive me, my love. I wasn't thinking. You're the
most valuable creature in my realm, I will take care that
no harm comes to you. You are the vessel of all my*

hopes, my beloved Gruoch.' His repetitious delight grew
wearisome very quickly, and I excused myself, claiming
I was overcome with emotion and needed to lie down.

But not before he'd insisted that we have a banquet
and that he send messengers to all the important figures
in Moray and beyond to invite them to celebrate with us.
That saved me the difficulty of trying to communicate the
news to Macbeth. I felt sure he would understand the
truth of the matter.

A month later, the compound was filled to bursting
with everyone who wanted to stay in Gille Coemgáin's
good books. Our quarters were piled high with gifts for
the baby. Once the guests were gone, I planned to
distribute most of the practical presents to the women of
the clan. It was as good a way as any to keep them on my
side if rumours were to start at any point.

I left Aife strategically making honey cakes with the
baker, keeping an eye on the entrance to the courtyard so
we'd know when Macbeth arrived. He brought only ten
of his men, a clear indication that he came in goodwill.
Aife excused herself and found me in the physic garden,
where I was using 'helping Eithne' as an excuse to be out
of the way. And also as a reminder to Macbeth of our
first private encounter.

'He's here,' she said, a little out of breath. 'And you've
never seen a better turned-out troop. Bright blue lèines
that look new, hunting jerkins buffed to a sheen, matching

calfskin boots too.' She grinned. *'If I didn't know better, I'd say he was trying to make a good impression.'*

I gave her a friendly buffet on the shoulder. 'If you should happen to cross his path, you might mention I'm down in the garden picking pot herbs for the banquet.'

She made a mocking bow and skipped off before I could take revenge. Eithne and I shared a smile, and I carried on picking the best of the sage leaves. I'd filled my basket and moved on to the thyme before a pair of polished riding boots stepped into my field of vision. I straightened up, a hand in the small of my back, and looked into those ice-blue eyes. His expression was more solemn than I'd expected. My heart thumped in my chest, and I felt faint.

'My lady Gruoch,' he said softly. *'I rejoice to see you again.'*

'Eithne, you should take the herbs up to the kitchen, the cook will need to season the meat soon.' Without looking away from Macbeth I blindly held out the basket. Eithne took it and we were alone again. *'My lord Macbeth,'* I said. *'Thank you for coming to share our celebration.'*

His eyebrows rose at my stressing the word 'our'. 'I wondered,' he said. *'I hoped.'*

'Does that please you?'

His face opened in a generous grin. 'I'm bursting with pride and happiness.'

I felt tears welling up. Pregnancy had stripped me of my stoicism and made me prone to all kinds of emotional outbursts that I struggled to hide. 'That is a relief. I feared you might not welcome the understanding.'

He shook his head. 'Gruoch, not a day has passed without thoughts of you filling my head. I have never missed anyone so much. I talk to you when I'm alone. I dream of you when I'm asleep. I have never felt like this about a woman before.'

He loved me. It was knowledge I had not dared hope for, but it was what I'd craved more than anything.

'It's been the same with me, Macbeth. Carrying your child feels like a blessing. It makes you a part of me that I can never deny.'

'I want to be with you,' he said. I couldn't quite credit the speed we were moving at. But we both knew we didn't have much time. We were still standing a distance from one another. Any watcher would only have seen a casual conversation between distant cousins.

'I think of that every day. There must be a way.'

He nodded. 'And we will find it. I do not want my child raised by Gille Coemgáin.'

I raised my eyebrows. 'That brute doesn't deserve the honour. Now, you must return to the hall. You've spent long enough congratulating me. Your absence will be noticed. Go, at once.'

He bowed low. 'Can I come to you tonight?'

'It's too dangerous: there are too many eyes. But soon, I promise.' I watched him leave through the herb plantation, a spring in his step, his hair bright as the very sun, his shoulders squared to carry the burden of whatever lay ahead.

He loved me.

By next morning our luck has dwindled. A fine smirr of rain wakes us, dripping from the leaves above. We all know from harsh experience how quickly we'll be soaked to the bone in weather like this. We hastily pack up and venture deeper into the woodland. 'We need proper shelter, Angus,' Ligach says. 'We'll not make it in this. The horses will soon tire and so will we.'

'We've not passed so much as a shepherd's hut for hours,' Angus says gloomily. 'But there's a settlement at the head of the loch. We can likely find shelter there.'

'How far is it?' Eithne asks.

'No more than a couple of miles,' he says. 'If we cover most of the ground now, I could go on ahead and see whether it's safe. Make arrangements for us all?' He looks to me for an answer; I am still his queen, I am expected to take decisions. I'd rather leave it to Eithne, to be honest, but there's no time for that.

'Let's do it.' What choice do we have? News travels slowly out here on the edges of the kingdom. It's hard enough trying to feed and house a family; there's no time to spend on frivolous visits to the neighbours. The few inhabitants are so widely scattered, they often don't hear what's happened in the next glen for months. Nobody from round here will be leaving their home ground till they move their cattle to better grazing in the spring. I can't believe the news of Malcolm's slaughter of Lulach and his snatching of the Scottish throne will have made it across these hills already. As far as anyone around Loch Earn will be aware, I am still the Queen Mother, Gruoch of the house of MacAlpin. When I have to, I can bury my grief and my fear and play that role.

So we weave through the trees, Angus's woodcraft sufficient to keep us more or less on track. When we reach the edge of the forest, we can see a huddle of houses and barns, one a shade bigger than the rest. I count them quickly; I make it thirteen cotts, three with thin threads of smoke rising through the roofs, four byres, what looks like a granary, a slow-turning watermill and the red glow of a smithy. The Big House is actually smaller than our barn at the monastery. There's no sign of any war band, not even an archery butt or a training dummy for swordplay.

'Considering they're on the very edge of the kingdom, they're not preparing for battle any time soon,' Ligach says.

'It's a wee bit out of the way here,' Angus tells her.

'When we turn north to A' Chrìon Làraich – that's the pass where the glens to the north and the west meet – it'll be a different story. That's where we'll have to watch out. News is as much currency there as siller.' He dismounts and we follow his lead, bending and stretching.

Aife pulls a face. 'How do you know all this stuff, Angus?'

He looks at me. 'Can I tell them?'

I shrug. Enough time has passed now for there to be no danger from the knowledge. I'll be surprised if he hasn't told Ligach. 'It's your secret, Angus. I don't think it has the power to hurt now.'

He casts a quick look at Ligach. 'I've never told, my queen. It wasn't my place.' Visibly he pulls himself together. 'When I was a boy, Macbeth chose me for a household servant and placed a special trust on me. He chose me to be the bearer of messages between himself and his kinsmen.'

'We know that,' Ligach says impatiently. 'That's how we got to know you.'

'But I was more than that. I didn't just deliver word to the likes of Gille Coemgáin. I carried the messages between Macbeth and my mistress, the queen.'

Ligach looks astonished. 'You never!'

'I did. Whatever passed between them for the best part of a year passed through my hands.'

Aife frowns. 'But I never saw you talk to her.'

Angus shrugs. 'I delivered messages in the language of flowers.'

Aife laughs in delight. 'How did none of us know about this? I thought we knew all your secrets, Gruoch.'

'And how did you avoid being caught out?' Eithne asks.

'The one place I could be without raising suspicion was the stables. I always made a fuss of my horse, all the stable lads knew that. I'd settle her down and talk to her till I was alone. My lady' – a nod to me – 'kept a game bag with a concealed pocket in the stables. It used to take less than a minute to swap my floral message for the one that was already there.'

They all gasp. And no wonder. It was an enterprise that could scarce have been more freighted with risk. But Angus had played his part with aplomb. I remembered Gille's groom sarcastically saying, 'That boy Angus'll never marry unless she's got four legs.'

'Macbeth told me he had a herbalist on Mull the first time we met. I knew then that he had someone who could translate the messages in the flowers.' My smile was tinged with sadness. 'And I had Eithne.'

Eithne was shocked. 'I thought you were genuinely interested.'

Wry, I said, 'For once, your intuition let you down, Eithne.'

She looked cross. 'So it goes when we know someone too well; we reject an instinct that runs counter to what we know of them.'

'It would only have endangered you if you'd understood

my reasons.' I turned back to our guardian and guide. 'I owe you a debt of gratitude, Angus.'

He shakes his head. 'No, I'm the one who owes you, my lady. All the lads I grew up with, they've had dull, predictable lives. I've had excitement and adventure. I've seen more of the world than any of them. From Rannoch Moor to Rome and back again.'

Ligach tousles his hair. 'And now it's time to explore the fleshpots of Loch Earn and find us food and shelter till the weather turns back in our favour.' She gives him a friendly skelp on the arse. 'Go on, get us sorted.'

He grins. 'I swear you sometimes think it's you that's the queen, Ligach.'

'No, she's just the queen of you,' Aife bats at his retreating back. We watch him go. 'We're lucky to have him,' she says, tucking her arm into Eithne's.

I can't help feeling a stab of jealousy. Ligach has her Angus, Aife her Eithne. But tonight I'll sleep alone, even if I'm tucked up alongside my women. It has been a long four years since Malcolm vanquished my king once and for all at Dunsinane. Empty bed, empty arms, empty heart.

We settle ourselves under the trees and Eithne gets out her runes. She has us all rapt, under the spell of her casting. She throws them once, then twice, then frowns. 'That makes no sense,' she mutters. 'The one contradicts the other. Like day and night.'

Aife leans in towards her. 'Maybe not a contradiction?

Maybe an order of events? Which comes first, my love? Day or night?' Her voice is gentle.

Eithne gives her a blank look. 'That's not how it works. They sit alongside each other in the runes. Time runs differently there, you know that, Aife.'

Ligach's lips tighten. She sometimes struggles with how Eithne sees the world. I understand that; I can't make sense of it either. The difference is that I don't feel the need to nail it down at all four corners as Ligach does.

She stirs herself and fetches her fishing rod from the slipe. 'I'm going to see what the burn has to offer,' she says, stomping off through the trees to the brook we can hear nearby.

Eithne seems dismayed. 'I wish she'd pay attention,' she mutters. 'It's not as if it doesn't affect her.'

'She doesn't want to know what's ahead of her,' I tell her. 'Ligach dwells not in the past or the future but in the here and now.'

'Poor Angus,' Eithne says.

I exchange a look with Aife that tells us both we have no idea why Angus is poor. At last he reappears on the other side of the rough ground between us, and 'poor' is the last word that comes to mind. He's almost skipping across, an elderly woman struggling to keep up behind him.

'This is Mhairi,' he announces, drawing the woman into our circle. 'She remembers when Macbeth became the Mormaer; he made a progress through the countryside.'

I remember it too. I was supposed to be in mourning for Gille. But at least I had wee Lulach as an excuse for my good spirits. He was less than six months old and such a good baby. The wet nurse said she'd never had so easy-going an infant in her care. And meanwhile, his natural father was busy establishing his right to the Moravian kingdom, so we could all three of us live in peace.

This old woman had seen my man in all his glory, and I know how impossible it would be to forget that. I produce my most gracious smile. 'Macbeth loved the west of the country best,' I lie easily.

'Mhairi here is a widow now. She has room enough to offer us shelter until the weather lifts,' Angus says, reaching for the halter of his horse. Then he frowns. 'Where's Ligach?' Stricken, he seems on the edge of panic.

'Gone fishing,' Aife says, then raises her voice in a shout. 'Ligach, get yourself back here! Your man is asking for you.'

'Aife, behave,' Angus explodes. 'She won't like that, and you know it.'

'We're not in the monastery now, Angus. You don't have to hide the fact that you're keeping Ligach warm at night whenever you get the chance.'

Mhairi is bemused by this banter, it's clear. I take her to one side. 'Pay them no mind, they're like children penned indoors for too long. Mistress Mhairi, as your queen, I thank you for your service.'

Ligach pushes through the trees to join us. She's caught nothing but she takes Aife's teasing in good part. We follow Mhairi to the steading, where some of her neighbours have found excuses to be outside in spite of the rain. The doors of the smithy and the mill stand open; they've both become surprisingly popular for a mid-morning. Mhairi waves to everyone and most wave back as we pass.

Her cott is hard by the nearest of the byres. As we approach, I hear a couple of cows lowing and the bleating of sheep. A dog is tethered near the byre door; it barely lifts its head from its paws as we approach. 'Not much of a watchdog,' Aife mutters.

'That's because I'm with you,' Mhairi said. 'If I wasnae, she'd about deafen you.'

She led us inside her home. No fire burned; it was chilly and dark, but at least it was dry. A straw mattress lay in one corner; a pair of stools and a badly carved chair sat around where I expected a fire might be. 'It's not much,' she apologised. 'No' fit for a queen.'

'Thank you,' I said. 'It's enough for us.'

'Would you like some mutton broth? The miller's wife aye has a pot on the go. I could get the boy to fetch some to you.' She's desperate to make us feel welcome.

'If it's no trouble, that would be very welcome.' They can ill afford such generosity, but Angus will find a way to repay it that will cause no embarrassment, I know.

Mhairi disappears and returns soon afterwards with a

stack of wooden bowls. Behind her comes a youth carrying a heavy iron pot. After a couple of days on the run, the smell coming off the broth goes round my heart like a hairy worm. The lad ladles out the soup and tries to hand the first bowl to Angus. Mhairi tuts, takes it from him and passes it to me, with a deferential nod. The lad looks surprised but carries on filling the bowls and giving them to Mhairi to distribute. I worry whether the lad will read anything into her action but tell myself I'm over-reacting. Even if she's told them who I am, there's no need for anxiety, not in these parts.

With full bellies, we women curl up together on the straw, Angus lying alone by the door, wrapped in his heavy woollen cloak. Ligach wove it for him from unwashed wool, so it stays as waterproof as it does on the sheep themselves.

It's the dog that wakes us.

Love could only lift me so far. In the days after Macbeth left, my happiness slowly leaked away. What use was love if he was far from me? What use was love if there was no prospect of it becoming an everyday state? If I bore a child that did not know his father, that would be another reproach for giving my heart to a man I could not hold in my arms.

'It's just as well you're with child,' Aife said darkly a couple of weeks after the grand celebration.

'What do you mean?'

'There's no joy in you, Gruoch, only grumpy complaint. Everybody knows women turn strange when we've a bairn in our bellies. In your case, it's giving you an excuse for being so far out of humour.'

I gave her a sour look. 'I can't help it. You know what ails me.'

'I do. But, Gruoch, you have to guard against others taking guesses at what might make you so morose. Macbeth dances on a table – you're so cheerful you forget to glower at Gille. Macbeth comes to celebrate – you glow like pregnant women are supposed to. Macbeth leaves – you're a walking thundercloud.'

She was right. And there were suspicious minds and vicious tongues among us. Disgracing the queen would open the door for someone else to sit on the throne next to Gille. Until my child was born, I dared not be called into question. And so I took on the appearance of a painted devil-may-care.

It about killed me.

But not for long. A few days into my forced cheeriness, I was keeping Eithne company in the herb garden when Aife sauntered over. 'You should pay a visit to the stables,' she said casually. 'I hear your mare is missing you.'

I frowned. What nonsense was that? My mare had never shown anything but utter indifference to me. She cared not a fig who was on her back. 'Have you been sitting in the sun too long, Aife?'

She rolled her eyes. 'Trust me, Gruoch. You need to get yourself off to the stables. Now.'

I struggled to my feet. 'I have no idea what's got into you, but if that's what it takes to get you back to yourself, I'll go to the godforsaken stables.'

There, I found a young man plaiting the mane of a sturdy mountain pony. I recognised the coat of arms worn on the badges of my lover's men. When he saw me, there was no disguising the look of relief on his face. He looked around, checking we were alone. 'My lady, my lord Macbeth has sent me.' My heart thudded in my chest as he fumbled in his jerkin and pulled out a crumpled posy of half-wilted flowers. He passed it across to me and I recognised the flowers of the wild garlic, as much by the smell as the shape. There were a couple of limp pee-the-bed and a few forget-me-nots, with their furry mouse-ear leaves.

I frowned.

'My lord says you speak the language of flowers.' He recited the words as if they were in a foreign tongue. Eithne, I thought, recalling his remarks about having a herbalist of his own.

He picked up a satchel concealed among the straw.

From it he withdrew a game bag, large enough for no more than a brace of small birds. He opened it and lifted a flap at the bottom. 'This is for you. You can leave it here in the stable, in your mare's stall. Conceal your return messages here. I will come as often as my lord can find excuses to send messages to Gille Coemgáin, and you may reply to him in kind.'

I was astonished. It was such a simple stratagem, but I had confidence that it would work. We all had our own game bags for the hunt, and nobody showed any interest in so plain a thing. I took a deep breath and thanked him. 'What's your name?'

'I'm Angus. My liege lord has told me I should consider you under his protection. If you were to command me, I would obey.'

I almost laughed at his sweet sincerity but I recognised that it was heartfelt. I left the stables in a lighter mood than I'd known for weeks. I struggled not to break into a run as I hurried back to the physic garden, where Eithne was patiently weeding. 'Eithne, I would become familiar with the language of plants,' I said.

She showed no curiosity; she always found it unsurprising when others shared her fascination with the natural world. 'I'll happily tell you what I know,' she said, straightening up.

I produced my crumpled nosegay and held it out to her. 'What does this say to you?'

She wrinkled her nose. 'Wild garlic symbolises unity and good fortune, but it also stands for patience. Milk-gowans are all about overcoming hardship. And forget-me-nots? Well, that's obvious; they say, "My love is true, don't forget me."' She took the flowers from me and studied the plant stem that bound them together. 'When the flowers are tied together, the plant that binds them can send a message too. This is mallow; it represents the sender consumed by love.' She smiled at me. 'Where did you get this?'

'I found it in the stables.' I took the flowers back from her. I was lifted up; all at once, the prospect I'd begun to think impossible opened before me like a promise fulfilled. Yes, the wait would be hard and full of danger. But the outcome would be worth every clench of fear, every bowel-loosening threat. I might not believe in myself, but I believed in Macbeth.

'So, to further my education, if you reciprocated these feelings, how would you respond?' I asked, sounding as casual as I could manage.

Eithne pondered for a moment. 'Dog daisies, for patience . . . Maybe primrose for eternal love, though it might be a bit soon for that.' She dug me in the ribs and said, her voice a tease, 'If it was you, you could send a purple orchid. You know, the ones that you get on boggy bits of the moorland. That stands for royalty, respect and admiration. Busy Lizzie, that says ardent love. Bluebells for unwavering affection.'

I rolled my eyes. 'You really can say what you mean with flowers.'

'I've barely started. Vetch says, "your presence eases my pain", Sweet Alison reveals immortal love, valerian is all about readiness.'

'And if I was tying a wee nosegay?'

'Gorse for Gruoch, and for love in all seasons.' I saw something start to dawn in her eyes. 'Is this—'

'I'm bored, Eithne. I'm pregnant and nobody will let me do anything. My brain needs something, and I found this wee posy and thought it might be interesting to know more about flower messages, that's all. So maybe you could teach me some more?'

The messages crossed between us at unpredictable intervals. Sometimes there would be two in the same week, sometimes it would be nearly three weeks between them. I lived for those days when Angus would come riding through the palisade into the courtyard. My women knew something was building between Macbeth and me, but even Eithne hadn't worked out the route of our communication. Sometimes it's useful to have a trusted companion whose head is in a different world.

Macbeth visited again in the summer, bringing a tribute from Mull's early oat harvest. It was not an obligation, everyone knew that. But he framed it as a gift in advance of the arrival of another mouth to feed. Gille

was flattered, of course; he welcomed any opportunity
for a feast.

And, of course, I welcomed the chance to take
Macbeth to my bed again. He took such tender care
towards me, treating my swollen belly with gentleness
and respect. He swore he loved my body even more now
I was with child; I teased him that he loved me more
because part of him was always within me. As before, we
took every care to make sure none of Gille's men or his
servants saw anything out of the way.

On the morning of his departure, I was surprised to
find him deep in conversation with Eithne in the herb
garden. When I approached, he laughed and said, 'We're
caught red-handed, Eithne. I have been talking to our
friend here about ways to make things easier for you
when you are birthing your baby. My herbalist on Mull
has sent me with a tincture of guelder rose that she says
will ease the violence of labour pains.' He produced a
small stone bottle from his jerkin. 'The guelder rose
grows more strongly on Mull than it does here.'

Eithne took the proffered gift. 'I've heard of this
crampbark tincture.' She smiled up at me. 'It's as well to
be prepared; it won't be long now.'

Macbeth bowed. 'I must be away.' We both knew he
dared not spend any more time with us. I watched him
leave with heavy heart. I wanted to believe there would
come a time when he would be able to stay, but I couldn't

*picture how that would come about. Shame on me for my
lack of imagination.*

I swim up from the depths of a dream that's already
vanishing as I surface. It's black as a pitch barrel in here.
Somewhere a dog is alternating between howling and
barking. I don't know where I am except that my women
are here. Then there's a sudden circle of scarlet and yellow
light as the door covering disappears in a sheet of flame.

I start up, untangling myself from limbs and furs, my
eyes adjusting to the glow. Someone slices the burning
deerskin from the doorway before the roof catches, but
now there's more light from flaming torches. Outside at
first, then inside. Angus scrambles to his feet but he's too
late. A claymore slashes across his face and he falls,
screaming. Ligach is on her feet faster than a speeding
arrow. Her dagger strikes Angus's attacker in the throat.
I stupidly think, *she learned from the arbalest*, before
another man takes his place and guts her before our eyes.

Shock freezes me where I crouch. Next to me, I hear
Aife cry, 'No, no more! We surrender to you.'

'Enough,' I shout, as imperiously as I can manage. 'I am
your queen. I am Gruoch.'

A new arrival. He has the air of a leader. Three others

crowd in behind him. 'I know who the fuck you are and you're no queen of mine or anybody else's. You're a woman on the run and there's a price on your head. A price I'm going to collect.' He glances down at Angus, who's making a noise like a stuck pig. Without a second thought, he unsheaths his claymore and cuts his throat.

I wish there was any point in swearing vengeance but I won't give him the satisfaction. 'What a man you are,' I say. 'They'll sing songs about how bravely you fought against a group of sleeping women.'

He takes two steps towards me. His breath stinks of fish and death. He raises a hand to slap me, but something makes him pause. 'No, better to leave you unmarked. Malcolm likes to hand out his own punishments.' He turns away and tells his men, 'Bind them tight and throw them over your horses. Then we ride like the devil's at our heels till we get to Ben More. We'll change horses at Cameron's farm. We can make Glencoe before morning.' His men exchange looks. They clearly don't agree but they aren't going to argue. I can't blame them.

Eithne is shivering with fear. *Don't let her have a fit now*, I think. This man won't hesitate to kill her too. We've had enough loss tonight; the last fragments of my heart will break along with Aife's if they take her too. I hug Eithne to me and say, 'We will not resist. Take us where you will. Malcolm and I share the same blood. He may pay your reward but he will not make us pay with blood.'

'Pretty words, crone,' the leader scoffs. 'It would be a foolish man who trusted a woman with your history.'

'What do they call you?' I ask, as they drag us to the door. Mhairi lies unmoving by the path in a pool of blood.

'My name is MacDuff.'

I've heard of him. The Mormaer of Fife: belligerent and coarse, a seeker after the main chance. They say, 'It taks a lang spoon tae sup wi' a Fifer,' so protective are they of what's theirs. I don't give much for our chances.

The men don't hesitate. They bind us, ankles and wrists, and dump us over the withers of their horses. It's easily done for this war band don't ride with full saddles, just a simple stuffed leather pad. I soon understand where the word 'nightmare' comes from; this hellish ride near shakes my bones loose from their moorings. I soon fall into a kind of daze; all I know is pain and grief and I can't move my thoughts or my senses beyond that. That's a kind of relief; it spares me from reliving the hellish murders of Angus and Ligach.

I've no idea how long this torture continues, but at last dawn finds us close to a small fort on a promontory of a high mountain. I'm damp with the horse's sweat and everything hurts, from my head to my feet. We ride into a muddy courtyard and MacDuff's soldiers throw us to the ground as if we're sacks of grain. 'Take them to the keep and untie them. Give them water and bread and lock them in,' MacDuff orders.

There's a little light from some arrow slits in the wall, enough to let me see the damage the night has brought. Eithne is a ghost of herself, her eyes hollow and blank. I don't know what she can see, but it isn't Aife or me. Aife's eyes are red from weeping, but I can see she's forcing herself not to let go now. We're ripped and torn inside, that much is clear. The four of us – Ligach, Eithne, Aife and me – have been together every day since we were wee lassies playing merrels and dice. Losing Ligach is beyond understanding. Of all my losses, this is the one that unmoors me most because the blame lies unswervingly at my door.

The bread they bring is hard as a stone and the water is brackish. I force myself to drink, and soak the bread to make it edible. But I can't keep it down and I throw up in the corner we've already used as a privy. Aife fares better. She gags but manages to fight it. Eithne ignores both bread and water.

'We should try to sleep,' I say.

Aife scoffs. 'Sleep? I never want to sleep again. I never want to dream what we saw in that hovel.' She wraps her arms around Eithne to stop her rocking. There's no room for me in that embrace. I wonder if Aife will ever forgive me for tonight.

I wonder if I will ever forgive myself. We set all this in motion, Macbeth and me. Love buoyed us up, made us ignore the stark realities of life and death. And this is where it has brought me. I have never been so alone.

Any woman will tell you that childbirth is painful beyond
words. 'It's as well the body has no direct memory of
pain,' Eithne said. 'Otherwise the world would be full of
only children.' Even with all of Eithne's knowledge and
the skills of the midwives among our clan, I nearly didn't
survive. It was as if my Lulach wanted to stay inside me,
that the flesh of my beloved didn't want to be untimely
ripped from my womb.

Truth to tell, I remember almost nothing of the
experience, mostly thanks to Eithne. She gave me
everything short of poppy to ease my agony. But even the
knowledge and experience of our women couldn't save
me from the damage that giving birth to my son caused
me. When Eithne broke the news that there would be no
more children for me, it felt like something my body
knew already.

Not that Gille cared. He had his son, his line was
secure. Or so he thought. He was determined to
celebrate the birth with another huge feast regardless of
my inability to walk without discomfort, never mind
dance. I made no attempt to talk him out of it; Macbeth
deserved to meet his son as soon as possible. And I pined
for the sight of him.

So our larders were emptied for a third time inside a year. I shuddered to think of how our people would endure the winter with so little left to sustain them. The cooks and bakers worked from before dawn till well after dusk to make the most of everything they had. They knew it was more than their lives were worth to produce a feasting board to celebrate Lulach that was anything less than memorable.

Eithne gave me some potion to see me through the banquet so none would guess the extent of my infirmity. But at the first sight of Macbeth striding into the hall, my heart jolted in my chest and everything except my love for him faded into the background. He made straight for the thrones where Gille and I were seated and spread his arms wide. 'Cousins!' he exclaimed. 'All honour to you for preserving the great line of Kenneth MacAlpin, our noble ancestor.' His war band applauded and cheered, and the rest of the room joined them.

'Now, where is this new prince, that I may swear my loyalty to him?' Macbeth looked around the room.

'He is in his cot, asleep,' Eithne said from behind my shoulder. 'Will you come with me, Lord Macbeth?

And off he went, long before I had done feasting on the sight of him. I did not think my eyes could ever have enough of him. I knew in my heart there were conversations he needed to have with my women, but it did not make it easier to see him walk away.

When Macbeth returned, Gille insisted he sit next to
him. So I was perfectly placed to hear the first links in
the chain of Macbeth's plan fall into place. 'You honour
us with another rich feast,' he began. 'And every
Moravian is proud to have an open-handed lord like Gille
Coemgáin standing over us.'

Gille nodded graciously. 'As they should be.'

'But, my lord, I have learned a practice on Mull that
I believe has a true part to play.'

Gille frowned. 'Is this some monkish quackery they've
fooled you with? I always said you listen too much to
those self-righteous pricks.'

'I take from them only what I find useful,' Macbeth
said. 'When they do this with sincerity, it has good
outcomes. When they do not . . . well, things don't
always turn out so well. Cousin, I want only the best start
in life for your son – who is also my cousin. And this will
cost you nothing.'

That caught Gille's attention. He only likes to spend
when it brings him benefits. 'So what is this nonsense?'

'It's simple. You must gather your men around you.
Only your men, your whole war band. Bring them here
to the hall. You come together to pledge your allegiance
to the new babe, and to the clan. You give thanks for the
birth and for Queen Gruoch, you ask for blessings on
them and you toast the future. Then it falls to your key
warriors to say something in praise of the house of Gille

Coemgáin.' Macbeth lifted his hands from his lap in a gesture that says, 'That's it.'

'And this works?' Gille's tendency to suspicion was not so easily allayed.

'I have seen it. If Lulach were my son, I would not hesitate. I would already have done it with my whole heart. It strengthens the clan as well as the child.'

'Will the men support it?'

Macbeth shrugged. 'If you command it, they will support it. What do you have to lose? You spend an evening drinking and praising and calling down blessings on the clan. If it brings good luck, you win. If not?' Another shrug. 'There must be some among your men you suspect of insincerity. They can carry the blame.'

Gille liked the idea of having ready-made scapegoats if he failed. I knew that would appeal to him. 'So it's really an excuse for a night's drinking without the women?'

Macbeth winked. 'You have it, cousin. With the bonus that, if all goes well, you can take the credit.'

Hook, line and sinker.

One thing I would have said for Gille – once he made his mind up to do something, he threw himself into it. Before Macbeth and the other guests had left, he was already planning the gathering of his war band. He chose the date of the next full moon, believing that to be a good omen. He ordered the brewer to have a supply of the finest barley bree and strong beer on tap for the ceremony.

*Eithne came to me and told me that she was part of
Macbeth's plan. His herbalist had joined the war band for
the birth celebration and the pair of them had discussed
what had to be done. They knew that the drink might
stupefy the men over time, but Macbeth needed
something swifter and more reliable. So Eithne mixed
her own version of dwale, a sleeping draught that's a
concoction of henbane, poppy and hemlock, flavoured
with rosehip syrup to soften the taste and sit well within
the bree and the ale.*

*I did not ask Macbeth what he planned. If he was
using me to climb to where his ambition pointed, I did
not want to know. I wanted to be able to trust his
motives. I wanted to believe in our love. I wanted nothing
to stand in the way of our future.*

*When the moon rose, the men walked into the hall,
full of curiosity for the ceremony that lay ahead. All fifty
of the Coemgáin war band filed in and settled down on
their benches, jugs of beer and bree on the tables in front
of them. None of them held back; warriors have to prove
their prowess at drinking as much as fighting.*

*The doors to the hall were closed behind them. As
Macbeth had explained, this was a ritual for the men
only. Time passed, and gradually the conversations inside
the hall stilled. We could barely make out Gille's raised
voice. Out of the shadows crept a dozen dark figures.
With silent stealth, they blocked the doors to the hall*

*with bales of hay and wooden settles. They poured pitch
over the kindling, then lit their torches and set fire to
the barricades.*

*Within minutes, the hall turned into a funeral pyre
from hell. Wood and thatch were no match for fire and
flame. At first there were screams, but not many, and not
for long. As the inferno died down, Macbeth stood before
the rest of the clan and delivered his message. 'Gille
Coemgáin murdered my father, Findlaich. Gille did it not
because of anything my father did wrong, but only
because he wanted to be Mormaer. He conspired with
Malcolm to murder Findlaich and divide the kingdom
between them. So now I have taken back the lordship that
should have been mine. I am your new Mormaer. And
you are my people, my clan. I promise you I will rule
with fairness. There will be no more tyranny in Moray.'*

*'What about the boy Lulach?' It's Angus, primed to
ask the question.*

*'I swear I mean no harm to Lulach. He has done me
no wrong. I stand here today and name Lulach as my
heir.'*

*There's a stunned silence, not least from me and my
women. We'd known something momentous was
coming; but we'd had no clue about the heirship. My eyes
filled with tears; the smoke was a perfect excuse to cover
my emotion. At that moment, I loved him all the more
for taking guardianship of our son.*

His eyes met mine, and he inclined his head towards
me. It was a promise I trusted.

Another gruelling day at the fastest pace the horses could
manage. I hear one of our captors say we'll stop for the
night at Onich. That makes sense. Malcolm is somewhere
at the far end of the Great Glen. MacDuff will use the
low-lying route to get us into my enemy's hands as quickly
as possible. Ironically, we'll have to follow the north shore
of a different Loch Leven. So far from St Serf's Isle and yet
no distance at all. It ties a kind of terrible knot.

We'd been so near to safety. Two or three more days
would have seen us on Mull, among loyal kinsmen.
Malcolm could not, would not have touched us there.
Instead, we're prisoners with no prospect of rescue since
nobody knows where we are or where we're bound.

At least the rain has stopped. The sun even broke
through the clouds for a while, but there was no heat in it.
Cold, stiff and sore, we could hardly move when we were
hauled off the horses for a break. The three of us huddled
together, nibbling on stale bannocks and stringy dried
venison. We had no appetite, but Aife insisted we eat to
keep our strength up.

'How much longer?' Eithne asked.

Neither of us responded. We both had a rough idea of where MacDuff was planning to take us, and it would be a few days' hard riding yet. The prospect was appalling.

I'd had enough. I reminded myself that I was still a queen, whatever MacDuff seemed to think. I struggled to my feet and at once one of the warriors had his claymore at my chest. I held my hands up in a gesture of surrender. I insisted on speaking to MacDuff and, grudgingly, the man let me pass.

MacDuff sat on a rock, gnawing a chicken leg. He looked up as I drew near. 'Why are you bothering me, woman?' he demanded.

'Malcolm will not thank you for delivering three broken women. You would do well to remember that Macbeth and me, we ruled Moray for seventeen years. We kept the peace, we were beloved. I was their queen and their queen mother. Treating us like traitors will not win Malcolm friends in Moray. He will understand the importance of that, even if it's beyond you.'

He scoffs. 'You think I should find a royal carriage around here?' He waves a derisive hand at the empty landscape.

'Untie us and let us ride. We can sit in front of your warriors. I give you my word that we will not attempt to escape.'

'Your word? The word of a woman who's been hiding behind the skirts of monks for years?'

I stare him out. If he thinks about this for a minute, he'll know I'm talking sense. We end up with a compromise. We can ride, but our hands will be loosely bound in front of us, not wrenched behind our backs. We're still captive, and I've given my word, but at least the last miles to Onich are more comfortable.

It's dark when we arrive, and the men take shelter in the ruin of a byre on the shores of the loch. We're consigned to what must have been a sheep pen or a pig sty further back along the inlet. We're fastened together at the ankles, our hands bound inside sacks to prevent us untying our bonds. We're not going anywhere; MacDuff is no careless fool, that much is clear.

Once the waning moon has risen, it casts enough light for us to see the ghosts of our faces. If I look as drawn as Eithne and Aife, no one from Gille Coemgáin's compound would recognise me. We are bedraggled and filthy as beldams. We smell disgusting too. All we need is a clowder of black cats to pass for witches.

Eithne and Aife fall into a fitful sleep, Eithne mumbling nonsense as she often does. I am too restless, beyond weary, tormented by visions of Angus and Ligach's last moments. I shift my position so I can stare down Loch Linnhe towards the sea. I came this way once, years ago, with Macbeth. He delighted in naming everything we passed – lochs, rivers, islands, mountains. This was the land where he'd grown to manhood. His father had spent much of his time in Ireland, but Macbeth and his mother stayed behind on Mull, Loch Linnhe his favourite fishing ground. His love for the island and its people was deep and abiding, and they loved him in return.

And here we are, a score of miles up the loch, so close and yet so far. My heart is sore; I doubt now whether I will ever set foot on Mull again.

As I stare, I imagine a moving dot on the horizon. I picture a high wooden stem breasting the water ahead of the single russet sail of a birlinn, a dozen oars helping its progress up the loch. I know it's a hallucination; there will be no rescue for us.

And yet . . . the more I gaze down the loch, the more real the fantasy war galley appears. But even if I'm not dreaming, the birlinn can have nothing to do with us. No one knows where we are or where we're heading.

I turn away, hoping sleep might finally take me. But now the snoring of the two men set to guard us is a loud counterpoint to Eithne's muttering. That Aife can sleep through it all is nothing short of a miracle.

When I swivel back to face the loch, I'm shocked to realise the birlinn is no ghost ship. It's much closer now, its sail swollen with the wind, the oars pulling in careful rhythm, barely splashing the surface. Her crew knows what they're about, that's clear.

As they draw nearer they change course to head into Kentallen Bay, bringing the boat round behind where we're camped. It's as if I was willing them on, the force of my desire like a magnet. Nobody else seems to be awake; whatever lookouts MacDuff has posted are insensible. It's not surprising, after the hard riding of the last couple of days.

And now they've dropped anchor close to shore, maybe half a mile up the beach from us. They silently ship the oars and I think I can make out bodies soundlessly slipping over the sides and into the shallows. I put my hand over Aife's mouth and shake her awake. She starts, eyes wide in fear. I turn her head in the direction of the birlinn and she struggles free, her expression bewildered.

Now the shadow shapes are heading down the shore, dark against the fringe of pale sand that lines the bay. As they draw closer, I struggle to my feet. If they're pirates, so be it. I'd rather be their captive than a pawn in Malcolm's kingdom.

They draw level with us, their faces blackened with soot. In the same instant, Aife and I both recognise the dead man leading the birlinn band.

It must be a delusion, brought on by the delirium of grief.

He creeps towards us, flanked by a pair of raiders. Aife's grip on my arm is like steel. My head is spinning, and it takes all my restraint not to scream my madness at the darkness.

And still the snores reverberate in the night.

But not for long. The raiders separate, their knives gleaming in the moonlight. Two swift slices across two throats, a long low gurgle and it's all over for our guards.

Now the leader turns to me, a ragged smile splitting his dark face. I'd know him anywhere. Macbeth has murdered sleep.

Aife yelps and I clamp my hand over her mouth. Meanwhile Macbeth's men are cutting us free, Eithne finally waking and looking up with a smile on her lips, as if this is what she's been waiting for. I step into my husband's arms and close my eyes in blessing, tears running down my face. None of this makes any sense, and I do not care.

There's no time for explanation or reunion. Macbeth sweeps me into his arms and the other two shepherd Aife and Eithne back to the shore. The rest of his crew escort us to the birlinn. Getting us aboard is much noisier than the landing had been, and as we push off from the shore, there are the sounds of alarum from the byre. Still, we're under way now, the sail raised and the oars manned. By the time MacDuff and his men have realised what's happening, we're moving out of the bay. A few of their arrows hit the high side of the hull, but they've been loosed from too great a distance and they bounce back into the sea.

And we're off, down Loch Linnhe towards the Sound of Mull. I'm dazed, beyond words. Beyond understanding. Eithne sits with her back to the mast, arms around her knees. 'I told you we had to go all the way west,' she said conversationally. 'I kept seeing Macbeth.'

'Why didn't you tell us?' Aife demands.

'I thought Gruoch would be angry. Because, you know, we all thought he'd died at Lumphanen.'

Macbeth joins us in time to hear this. 'I'm sorry for the lie. I was grievously wounded at Lumphanen, near death when they carried me from the battle. The MacNeil had me taken to one of his strongholds on Skye. The word spread that I hadn't survived.' He smiles, the familiar crooked grin. 'Being dead kept me alive. You can't kill off a dead man.'

'Why didn't you tell us?' Aife demands, fierce as ever. 'We would never have betrayed you.'

He shakes his head and sighs. 'I was very ill for a long time. Too ill to make decisions. Then, I didn't want to put you in danger. Your honest reaction added weight to my version of events. If anyone had doubted that, you could have been taken hostage. I needed to wait till Lulach was secure on the throne, then we could have been reunited on Mull. Before that, letting Malcolm know I was alive would have been signing a death warrant for all of us. That snake believes I'm the only man capable of dethroning him. And besides, I was in no fit state to mount a raid, never mind lead an army,' Macbeth admits. 'I almost died twice after I nearly died on the battlefield.'

'Did you have a good apothecary?' Eithne asks.

'The second-best,' he says, bowing to her. 'Now, you

must make yourselves comfortable. We have a long sail ahead of us.'

'Surely not?' Aife points in the vague direction of Mull. 'We'll be there in no time.'

Macbeth shakes his head. 'Mull will be too dangerous for us for some while now. I have found a new sanctuary for us. The MacNeil has come to our aid again. Tonight we sail for Caisteal Chiosmuil.'

'Where's that? Is it in Ireland?' Aife asks.

'It's a fort in the mouth of Barra's harbour.'

'I'm none the wiser,' she complains.

Macbeth grins. 'It's at the bottom of na h-Eileanan an Siar. The Western Isles. We'll be safe there.'

'But that's Viking territory now! How——' Aife again.

'Later, Aife. Rest now.' My heart sings to hear that firm tone in Macbeth's voice. He's lost none of the power of command that made our reign so peaceful. He steers me away from the other two and we find a space at the stern.

Now the shock has passed, a different emotion is raging through me. 'You let me believe you were dead. How could you be so cruel? My heart broke. My spirit nearly broke. If I hadn't had my women at my side . . .'

He pulls me into his arms. 'I was trying to save your life, Gruoch. When I was well enough to understand what was being said, the MacNeil told me you were in sanctuary with the Chaldean monks. Nobody knew where to find you. My heart was breaking too. Without you . . . No chance to protect Lulach, to advise him . . . I failed you both.'

I push away from him. 'You succeeded in that at least. Not a day passed when I didn't suffer the pain of loss. Not a day has passed without my mourning your absence. Lulach would still be alive if you'd been there to steer his course.'

He nods, shame in his eyes. 'I know. And not a day will go by when I don't reproach myself for all you've suffered. I can't bring my boy back. I can't make it up to you. I can't change the past.' He lifts his head, his expression beseeching. 'I still love you with every beat of my heart, Gruoch.' A crooked half-smile. 'And I did rescue you.'

In spite of my determination to make him suffer something of my pain, I can't help myself. Macbeth is still the only man I have ever loved. And it feels as if I am condemned never to escape that. 'How did you know where we were?'

'Angus.' He sighs. I've already told him how we lost Angus and Ligach. 'He was the best of men. He had an arrangement with the son of the farm at Loch Leven. On the word from Angus that you were on the run, heading for Mull, the lad took off on their fastest horse and made for the MacNeil. He knew the time had come for me to resurrect myself, so he sent their fastest birlinn for me. We worked out which route you'd likely take. It was pure luck that we caught up with you at Onich. Our plan was to make camp at the head of the loch and wait for you to turn up. I didn't know MacDuff had captured you. Though I'd have welcomed the chance to take him on, Gruoch. It was him that nearly did for me at Lumphanen, not Malcolm. I've been ready for a return bout for a few months now.'

I stop his mouth with a kiss. 'I forbid it, Macbeth. All I want now is a peaceful life with you. No more battles. No more loss. I beg you.'

He pulls me closer. 'I'm so sorry about our son.'

I sigh. 'My poor sweet boy. I'd been afraid for him ever since you . . . ' I shake my head. 'He was born a follower, not a leader. Without your example to learn from, he was lost.'

'I'm so sorry. You'll never understand how much I regret the time we spent apart.'

I take a deep breath. I want to think about the future, not the past. What I can change, not what I can't. 'Tell me about Caisteal Chiosmuil. Is Aife right? Isn't that part of the King of Norway's fiefdom?'

He kisses me. 'It is. The raiders came a long time ago and settled there. Caisteal Chiosmuil's a tiny isle in the bay. Three cottages and a small byre, freshwater wells and a wee pier. It takes a matter of minutes to row to the shore. We'll be safe there, I promise you. It will be our new home. And if Aife and Eithne want to be more social – or more solitary – we can find them a place on Barra itself.'

If this is how my story is to end, I think I can bear it.

There was little dissent when the flames died down. Our people knew enough of Macbeth to take him at his word – or at least until he proved them wrong. Of course, there was grieving – Gille's men had wives and lovers and children bereft. But Macbeth was canny enough to pay blood money. It didn't hurt that his men gently reminded those left behind of Gille's ruthlessness and cruelties, and the connivance of their men.

From the start, we made choices that led to peace and prosperity. Macbeth ruled by consent; he settled disputes with other Moravians and our neighbours not by warfare but by inviting them to parley. Always under the roof of the magnificent new hall he had built. It was grand enough by itself to inspire awe; and our war band were always in evidence in the background, kitted out in the best of gear, weapons and smiles gleaming.

Early on, the Mormaer of Fife, MacDuff, tried an incursion into our territory. Macbeth hung back, letting MacDuff think he was too nervous of failure to stand against him. Late one night, when the moon was dark, Macbeth's men stole into MacDuff's camp. Half of his war band were dead or as good as before anyone even knew Macbeth's men were on their ground. It was a short and effective skirmish, and that

was the last we heard from Fife other than the
occasional episode of cattle rustling. Cattle rustling is a
kind of hobby to those Fifers, after all. They steal
the beasts; we take them back. It follows the same
broad rules as our dances.

Some say Macbeth should have killed MacDuff that
night. But he knew that would only lead to another blood
feud. And he knew what the outcome of a blood feud
would be. Better that MacDuff's sons and his wife fled
south into the arms of Malcolm and his supporters, telling
their tales of the terrible reach of Macbeth's war band.

The only real threat to our reign turned into a unique
opportunity for its expansion. Our distant kinsman
Duncan had slaughtered his way to the throne of Alba,
but that wasn't enough to satisfy him. He wanted Moray.
He moved against us, and we ended up facing his army in
a bloody battle near Elgin. Macbeth killed him in single
combat, so Duncan's kingdom of Alba fused with our
Moray. We called the joint kingdom Scotland.

Some of the defeated army tried to spread a rumour
that Macbeth had murdered Duncan in his sleep, but
there were too many witnesses on the battlefield for that
story to grow legs. The former kingdom of Alba chose
the road of friendship and unity because they saw the
Moravians had more secure lives than they had.

We made our peace too with the Christians. And the
Chaldeans. Not a pretence of peace, but a genuine

commitment to working together. 'Men have to believe in something,' Macbeth said. 'One superstition is as good as another. Our people like that their Christ suffered as we suffer. The monks make good mead and honey, and the books they make of their gospels are beautiful.' And so we all became Christian, their churches and monasteries part of our compounds.

All of this only made Macbeth and me more popular. The women liked that there was much less fighting and more farming. So did the men. The occasional skirmish on our borders kept the war band sharp, but the casualties were few. Eithne's skills grew stronger, so the outcomes for the wounded were better.

And me? I was content but not complacent. The better I came to know Macbeth, the deeper my love grew. Our passion never diminished either; we never lost sight of the joy of being lovers as well as partners and friends. My women, who had learned to live with anxiety for my fate and therefore theirs, relaxed. Ligach became the most skilled of all our weavers, teaching young women how to produce decorative and useful fabrics. Eithne's physic garden grew larger and more varied, her ointments and medicaments more diverse and more potent. And Aife? Aife did what Aife did best, making herself unobtrusively invaluable. It wasn't perfection, for there are always stones in the road. But we lived our lives the best we could.

If there was any drawback to the security of our kingdom, it was that our son never had the chance to learn to be a leader of men. Lulach was softer than his father had ever been; he'd never had the need either to fight or to persuade. Macbeth did his best to train him in combat, but it was clear to me that the boy didn't see the point. Macbeth tried to hide his disappointment. But I could see it and tried to make it up to the boy.

Almost ten years after we had unified Moray and Alba, the abbot of St Serf's Isle in Loch Leven arrived with half a dozen of his monks. Macbeth made him welcome not with a grand feast but with a private dinner showing the best of our fine larder. Meat, game, fish, cheese, sweetmeats and three kinds of bannock. The monks ate like men half-starved.

'Your creation of Scotland has brought peace to our lands,' the rosy-cheeked abbot said, folding his hands over his rounded belly.

'From which we all benefit,' I said. 'Men, women and children.'

He looked surprised at my contribution. I supposed those nuns he encountered had little to say for themselves. I'd heard many of them had taken vows of silence; that was one way to deal with the pompous and the arrogant. 'Indeed, my queen,' he agreed, a little stiffly, before turning to Macbeth. 'We wanted to suggest something to mark your time as King of Scotland.'

Macbeth raised his eyebrows. 'What did you have in mind? There's not much that we lack here.'

'My lord Macbeth, you are rich in worldly goods, and your generosity is well known. But it never hurts to make provision for what comes after.'

Macbeth exchanged a look with me, one corner of his mouth twitching almost imperceptibly. 'That's an interesting notion, abbot. Though there is no way to demonstrate how effective that'd be.'

Not in the least disconcerted, the abbot inclined his head and said, 'That's where your faith comes in.'

'What did you have in mind, abbot? Have we not been generous enough to St Serf's already, endowing the land and supplying the stone for your monastery?'

'You misunderstand me,' he said, almost huffy. 'I had in mind a pilgrimage. To Rome.'

A stunned silence. None of us had expected that. 'That's madness,' Aife broke in from the far end of the table. 'It's hundreds of miles away. Dozens of days of riding. Hundreds, maybe. You can't leave the land for that long, my lord.'

The abbot tutted. 'My lady, there is more than one way to travel. It takes less than three weeks by sea.'

'That would still mean we'd be gone for at least two months,' Macbeth said. But I could see the faraway look in his eyes that I was accustomed to whenever a difficult dream offered itself up to him. I'd seen it first in Eithne's herb garden years before, and I couldn't complain about where that had taken me.

He changed the subject, but I knew the abbot had planted a seed that would grow into a fully-fledged plan. That night, our love-making was fierce and wild, and it was no surprise to me that afterwards he said, 'I should like to see Rome. I've heard it takes the breath away. And two months is not so long.'

'Dare you leave our lands for two months?'

'I can leave the MacNeil as regent. The men respect him, and even MacDuff would hesitate to go against him in the field, I think . . .'

His words pierced me. 'Do you not trust me to stand in your place?'

He looked astonished and let out a great guffaw of laughter. 'You would be with me, Gruoch. At my side. Did you really think I could leave you behind on such a great endeavour?' He rolled back on top of me, gripping my shoulders tightly. 'Do you not know me at all? How could I bear to be separated from you again?'

And it no longer seemed such a bad idea.

Rome was a revelation to us. From the moment we landed in the bewilderingly busy port of Ostia, I felt we'd stumbled into a dream. There on the quayside we came face to face with our cousin Thorfinn, Yarl of Orkney and Macbeth's man in Caithness. We knew he'd planned to make a pilgrimage to Rome, but he'd left months earlier and we'd had no word since.

The two men fell into each other's arms like long-lost brothers. 'Where have you been all these months?' Macbeth demanded, holding him at arm's length. The only change in the familiar giant black-haired Viking was that he'd become as sun-browned as the local Romans; except for his prow of a nose, which glowed red as a fire-coal.

'I took the land route,' Thorfinn said. 'I travelled down through Saxony. I spent time making friends with the Holy Roman Emperor. Henry is a shrewd man; who knows what his intentions are towards the English? But it will do us no harm to have an alliance with him.'

Macbeth clapped him on the back. 'You never rest, Thorfinn. It's good to see you, man!'

Thorfinn had already secured rooms for us and our men by the Pons Antonius bridge across the river Tiber, near the Capitoline Hill. We travelled across the city in a cart on a miraculously flagged road, wondering at the sights and sounds and smells of a city that made our compound shrink to insignificance by comparison. Everywhere stood mighty stone buildings, some of them in a parlous state of disrepair, others with impressive pillars and carvings. Statues seemed to spring from the very pavements. Everywhere there was hustle and bustle, the constant buzz of conversation and the cries of hawkers and tradesmen. I had never seen anything like it.

*We soon learned how easy it was to tell where people
stood in society by the quality of clothes they wore. From
senators to slaves, each rank was clear. We were
hopelessly overdressed, our wool and animal skins far too
warm for the sunny climate. We had to buy some tunics
and robes to avoid heatstroke.*

*At first, we were shocked at the idea of slavery: the
notion that one human could own another was foreign to
us. But we soon understood that the Romans found our
clan system equally bewildering.*

*The food was as alien as the social divisions.
Everything came slathered in sauces, flavoured with alien
spices and herbs. Aife and Eithne would disappear for
whole days and return with jars of oil and strange sauces
that filled our mouths with unfamiliar sensations. We ate
all sorts of fish and seafood we'd never seen before. But
what truly overwhelmed us were the sweet fruits and
candied nuts that filled platters at the end of meals.*

*We also discovered on our first evening that beer was
unthinkable. 'Barbarian,' the taverna owner exploded
when Macbeth asked for a jug of ale to cool him down in
the heat. We had to learn to enjoy wine at every meal,
mixed with water and yet more spices. It was no
hardship . . .*

*Thorfinn was our enthusiastic guide, and together we
explored the ancient city as well as performing the sacred
offices required of a pilgrim. Towards the end of the*

second week, the word came that we had secured an
audience with the Pope himself.

I had been hearing about Pope Leo IX for days. He'd
been the bishop of a frontier town, so he'd had to deal
with attacks on his province. As well as being a warrior,
he'd had to be a diplomat, and also to shepherd his flock
through famine. 'Sounds like one of us,' Macbeth had
said. 'A man of peace who knows how to handle a sword.'

'Not exactly like us,' Thorfinn slung back at him.
'He's a stickler for celibacy.'

'Aye, but only for the clergy,' I said. 'Not for
red-blooded men like you.'

The Lateran Palace, where the Pope lived, was on the
other side of the city from our lodgings. We passed
through gardens, through markets, past street stalls
selling food and drink, clothes and sandals; it felt as if we
were passing up and down all of the seven hills that they
say Rome is built on. The more I saw of the city, the
more I wanted to see.

The palace itself must be one of the wonders of the
world. I didn't have the words to describe it then, and I
still don't. I was overwhelmed by the beauty of the room
where we met with the Pope, by its mosaics, its
paintings, its gold and silver caskets for various relics of
saints. (Not that I believe in the magical powers of bits of
dead bodies; I leave that to Eithne!) One hall even had a
massive fountain in the middle, indoors. I began to

understand how small was the world Macbeth and I had
fought to make our own.

Pope Leo himself did not live up to his palace.
Underneath his rich red and gold robes, I could see he
was a slight figure of a man. His features were fine, his
eyes bright, but it was hard to read his expression since
the lower half of his face was covered with a thick grey
beard. He seemed to have no idea who we were or
where we had come from. He blessed us in Latin, and we
stooped one by one to kiss his foot. I thought Thorfinn
would refuse, but at the last moment he bent and
touched his lips to the papal slipper.

We were ushered out almost before we could catch our
breath. I felt no sudden surge of spirituality, no sense of
being more blessed than I had been before. Even Eithne
was apparently unmoved by the encounter. All I felt was
respect for a man who had managed to rise to such a
position of power and to hold on to it. Later, when the
men had gone out drinking, I asked my women what they
had made of it. Eithne pointed to a large leather bag filled
with roots and seeds for plants she'd never seen before.
She'd made friends with local apothecaries, some from as
far away as Jerusalem and Marrakesh. 'I've learned so
much,' she said. 'But I'm wearying for home now.'

She said what we all felt. The following morning,
Macbeth announced that he and Thorfinn were going to
Ostia to arrange our voyage home. We'd fulfilled our

duties as pilgrims, we could assure the abbot we'd been blessed by the Pope, and we'd enjoyed the wonders of Rome. We had arrived in a spirit of utility, not faith, and we left in the same state.

A few weeks later, the MacNeil was waiting at the gates of the palisade to welcome us. 'Stands Scotland where it did?' Macbeth enquired.

His regent bowed. 'Aye, my king. Even stronger. The harvest's in and it's a good one. Our borders are secure, and all's well.'

So we settled back into our familiar patterns. Rumours reached us from the south that Siward, the Earl of Northumberland, was restless and determined to expand his territory. Macbeth summoned more of his young men to the war band and spent long hours training them in how to fight an enemy on land we knew best. But it soon transpired that Siward's ambitions lay elsewhere. His men moved south and west of his fiefdom, to shires that lay under the rule of other Scandinavian lords. And we slept easy in our beds again.

More fool us.

The sunset splashes colour across the western sky as we sail into the harbour where Caisteal Chiosmuil stands sentinel.

I soon learn that sunsets are always the best part of the day here, the sky filling with pink and gold and blue and purple and all the shades between.

The birlinn drops anchor by the short pier and we climb ashore. Macbeth told no lies when he described the steading, though the three cottages are more substantial than I expected. The byre too is twice the size of the one we called home on St Serf's Isle.

'What do you think?' Macbeth asks, a trace of worry creasing his brow. 'Can we be happy here? One cottage for us and our servants, another for Aife and Eithne and her potions, and the third for those who will work the land.'

With a pang of sorrow, I think that Ligach and Angus should have been the tenants of that third cottage. But I put my regrets to one side and raise a more immediate concern. 'But Vikings? Can we trust them? Will they trust us?'

'Our old friend Thorfinn has cleared a path for us; he holds sway here. They hate Malcolm even more than we do.'

We walk up to the houses. Built from solid granite blocks, they each have four rooms; it'll serve us well. I worry that we might not find enough to occupy us, then comes a stab of guilt. All those years I longed for Macbeth to come back to me, and now I'm wondering if he's enough for me. I hear Ligach's mocking voice in my ear: 'For shame, Gruoch, you lucky besom.'

Aife bounds across the threshold of the smallest cottage. 'Come and see, Eithne. It's even better than we had before

Lumphanen.' Eithne follows her, though without her usual ardour. I'm sure she'll recover her energies once she's established a proper physic garden and moved past the fear that has so distracted her since we fled St Serf's, and her anguish at the loss of Ligach.

Coming together with Macbeth has been a fresh dawn. This new life on Caisteal Chiosmuil is like a reawakening after a second sleep. The time apart that felt at first like a gulf has gradually shrunk to insignificance and we are closer than ever before. I can almost forgive the torture of believing him dead for the joy of finding him alive.

I wish I could say the same for Aife and Eithne. They spend more time apart than they do together. Eithne is preparing the soil and planting the seeds she kept on her person after we made our escape. She's not bitter about the irreplaceable botanical treasures she lost when MacDuff abandoned our baggage, and she works tirelessly to build her store of ointments, tinctures and herbal cures. Word of her skills spreads quickly, and soon the Norse come across the harbour to seek her help. They're brusque and nervy at first, but they soon settle. But Eithne's eyes are haunted by what she can't unsee. And I can't remember the last time I've seen her cast the runes.

Aife's interests lie elsewhere. She has made friends on Barra, both among the men and the women. She's learned the best places for hunting and fishing, and she spends most of her days filling our larder with fresh meat and fish, or curing and smoking what she has brought home. Lately, she's taken to hunting with Eivar, one of the Norse women. It's good to hear Aife laugh again.

Everything changes on a blustery day in the spring of our second year on Caisteal Chiosmuil. The farm lad from Loch Leven arrives on a birlinn from Mull. Malcolm is on the move again, he tells us. He's determined to become king of all Scotland. Word is he even thinks he can drive the Vikings out.

'Nobody believes he can do that. But you have friends on Mull and in Glencoe. They should be warned to be vigilant,' he tells us.

Eithne is stricken by his news. She hurries from our cottage to take refuge in her room of herbs. Aife watches her go, her sorrow evident in her face. 'She takes things so personally,' she sighs. 'It's as if by seeing it in her head, she blames herself when it happens.'

I should have paid more attention to Aife's words. The morning tide washes Eithne's body up by the pier. Her gathering bag is strapped across her body, and it's filled with stones.

Aife is inconsolable. 'I couldn't reach her,' she mumbles into my breast as I hold her close as once I used to hold Lulach. 'She was lost in her own world. She kept coming back to her part in the death of Gille Coemgáin and his men. "Everything bad came from that," she said. And now they're all dead – Ligach, Angus, Lulach, all the battlefield dead.'

'She didn't make it happen,' I tell her.

She pulls away, face wet with tears. 'You think I don't know that? You think I didn't tell her that every day?' Grief has sharpened her tone. 'You think I don't carry the guilt? Imagine for a moment that Macbeth understood the burden of his actions, really grasped what he put you through. How would you feel if that was his body washed up on the shore?'

I'm no stranger to thoughts like these, but I've always kept them locked away. I am a queen; they have to be able to look to me for guidance. A queen has to stand strong, above the devastation. A queen has to be the future, not the past. I draw Aife close again, but I know it means little to her. That fire that warmed and lit up all of us has gone out. Once we were four; now we are two, and the glue that held us fast has crumbled. Aife is not the only one whose tattered heart hurts.

Later, I turn to Macbeth as we wait for sleep. I tempt fate one last time. 'I have a plan,' I say

We woke one morning to the news that Siward and Malcolm had marched north with a sizeable army. Our outriders told us that his endeavours in the south had not brought him the successes he craved and the English king

had warned him off. So he'd decided Scotland was an easier plum to pick.

Macbeth rode out with his strongest war band; every man who could wield a sword, a bow or a spear rallied to his call. Under cover of darkness, the forward party arrived on horseback outside Siward's camp at the Seven Sleepers by Dunsinane and attacked. It was a fierce battle, no quarter asked or given. Siward suffered the worst personal losses early in the fighting. Not only did his son Osbjorn die; so did his heir, his sister's son Sigurd. His grief acted as a spur to his own battle rage, and although we managed to hold our kingdom that day, we had lost many of our best warriors.

We knew Siward would return. Our outriders reported that he was making further alliances. Malcolm, of course, was still his lapdog. But MacDuff had also joined Siward's cause. Macbeth knew we were outnumbered but he was determined not to yield. Our entire kingdom lived on the edge of alert for months, waiting for Siward's grief to manifest itself as battlefield fury.

It happened on Saturday, 15 August, a date I will never forget. The two sides clashed in a wood at Lumphanen; it was little more than a skirmish, with both main armies some distance away. But it was enough for Siward to strike what he thought was a fatal blow to my beloved husband.

Macbeth's men formed a phalanx round his body, bravely fighting off the enemy. They used the cover of the woodland to escape with his body and spread the word that he was dead. Siward had triumphed and Malcolm was hailed King of Scotland, third of that name.

The MacNeil rode personally to my side to break the news that Macbeth had been mortally wounded on the battlefield. I was mad with grief, but the ever-practical Ligach took note of my husband's final instructions, that I should flee with my women and Angus to the Chaldeans at St Serf's and demand sanctuary. It was a plan we'd made after Dunsinane, not really believing we would need it.

We were good at plans; but this was one I never wanted to execute.

I'm looking out across the water. I sometimes think if I added up the hours I've spent gazing across water I'd have a whole second life. My childhood, staring down the Moray Firth, learning to tell one dolphin from another. The river that ran past Gille Coemgáin's palisade. The lochan next to our stronghold as Mormaer of Moray then King and Queen of Scotland. Loch Leven, my place of exile with my women. And now the harbour of Barra. Beyond it, to the west, the mighty ocean leading to the edge of the world and Tír na hÓige, the mythical land of eternal youth and beauty where I like to imagine Eithne dwells.

Macbeth touches my shoulder. I hadn't been aware of his approach, which is strange because I usually sense it. I lean back against him. 'Are you ready?'

'I've made my farewells.' I turn to face the shore, where a birlinn is casting off and making towards us. A dozen volunteers at the oars, each a seasoned warrior, all of them young strong and single. It's too late now for any of us to change our minds.

The boat draws alongside, and we board. I check that the furs and supplies are loaded; Macbeth checks the weapons and the gold. At the last possible minute, Aife comes trotting down the path and leaps aboard. She is to travel with us as far as Malin Head, the very tip of Ireland. From there she will find a convent. I was taken aback at this proposal; I had never considered Aife a candidate for a life of contemplation.

'I've come to understand that it's all that's left to me without Eithne,' she says. 'I'll pray for the pair of you counterfeit Christians.' Her smile takes any harshness from the words.

We set sail at the turning of the tide. I take a last look at the familiar contours and colours of my native land, then I turn my face to the open seas.

We are bound south, for Rome, for warm winters and

sweet wine. We have letters from the Bishops of the Isles and Aberdeen, commending our generosity to the church and our humble piety. The bishops remind His Holiness of our previous pilgrimage and ask him to assume the role of our protector in Rome.

We will be safe there, I believe. I know I have thought myself safe before, but even if our enemies discover where we are, they must realise we offer no threat. A pair of deposed monarchs in exile with no army at our back; Siward and Malcolm will have enough to occupy them in their unruly realms to bother with vengeance. Theirs is the power now, but ours is the glory.

We were born into a land riven with petty feuds and ambition, and we united it under one banner and called it Scotland. And by the end, we'd created an object of envy that we couldn't hold on to. So we say farewell to the beloved country; we can be proud that we leave it stronger and richer than we found it. Who can say whether it was worth the cost?

Later, once we settle, we'll entrust Macbeth's closest attendant with one final task. When Macbeth dies, his heart should be removed and returned to Mull for burial in his own lands. I care not where I am buried; my divided heart will always lie with Macbeth, with Lulach and with my women. And with poor faithful Angus, whose unfailing loyalty set our story in motion and whose blood paid our ransom. For blood will have blood.

Glossary

auld	old
bannock	a round flatbread made from oatmeal, flour and buttermilk, cooked on a griddle or a cast-iron pan. Usually cut into quarters, split and spread with butter.
barley bree	a primitive form of whisky
beldam	an assertive older woman
besom	an assertive younger woman
bide, biding	to reside or remain
birlinn	a small galley or longboat with a single sail and oars
bleezing	bragging, showing off
bonnie, bonny	beautiful, attractive
braies	breeches
bunnet	flat cap, Tam O'Shanter
cac-shiubhal	diarrhoea (Gaelic)
canny	careful, considered

chaps	knocks
drop spindle	a simple and portable method of spinning yarn
druimean	Mid-Perthshire Gaelic for hill ridge, the source of the place name Drymen
dugs	breasts
fechter	fighter, warrior (bonnie fechter: admirable fighter)
fidchell	chess
filidh	bard
girnie	peevish, complaining
houghmagandie	sexual intercourse
jessies	weak or cowardly males
lèine	linen tunic
machair	low-lying grassland
madder	a herbaceous plant that produces a red dye
merrels	a board game also known as Nine Men's Morris
milk gowans	dandelions
Moravian	a person from Moray
Mormaer	leader, ruler
pee-the-bed	dandelion
pile wort	lesser celandine
pintle	penis
pottage	thick soup or stew of meat/fish/vegetables/legumes

ramsons	wild garlic
siller	money (from 'silver')
Slàinte mhath	'Good health' – a traditional Gaelic toast, to which the reply is 'Slàinte mhor', meaning 'Great health'
slipe	sledge or a drag
smirr	a fine, penetrating rain
zibeline	the fur of the sable

Acknowledgements

I'm grateful to Jamie Crawford and his colleagues at Birlinn for giving me the opportunity for such a fascinating gig. So much of Scottish history has been twisted into narratives that bear little relationship to the truth, and the story of Lady Macbeth and her husband is one of the more egregious examples of that. I hope this little book gives a more authentic picture of one of the most stable reigns of medieval Scotland.

Thanks are due to my in-laws, Mary and Paul Willcock, who lent us their apartment in southern Spain while I immersed myself in the past. It was certainly the warmest writing room I've ever had, and a view of the sea is always a fillip to my process!

Thanks also to Jo Sharp and Nicola Sturgeon whose animated dinner conversation resolved an awkward plot point for me. It's amazing how a few glasses of red wine release the imagination . . .

I'm grateful to Matt Lewis's endlessly informative podcast, Gone Medieval, which sent me down an entire warren of rabbit holes. And to Janina Ramirez's encyclopaedic *Femina*, a fascinating journey into the lives of women in the Middle Ages.

Thanks to the team at Birlinn for all their hard work to make this happen. And thanks too to Anne O'Brien, whose copy-editing I have learned to lean on over many years!

I owe much more than that to Jo. Her belief in me is what keeps me going over the next hurdle. She picks me up when I fall down and always encourages me onwards. More than that, she makes me laugh – at myself, and at the rest of the world.